ıns are up t
returned by
ıe L   ar
ıes.

IMPETUOUS HEART

What secrets does Beaumont Island hold? Attracted to its owner, widower Beau Powers, and his small daughter who is blind, local reporter Paula Bannister seeks answers. Though warned to drop her investigation, Paula needs to find the truth if her relationship with Beau and his daughter is to grow. But in delving into the mystery she endangers the lives of the two people she has grown to love and threatens any chance she has of happiness.

Books by Jo James
in the Linford Romance Library:

CHANCE ENCOUNTER
THE RELUCTANT BACHELOR
SHADOWS ACROSS THE WATER
SECRET OF THE RIDGE
AN UNEASY ARRANGEMENT
MYSTERY AT BLUFF COTTAGE

JO JAMES

IMPETUOUS HEART

Complete and Unabridged

LINFORD
Leicester

First published in Great Britain in 1998

First Linford Edition
published 2005

British Library CIP Data

James, Jo,
    Impetuous heart.—Large print ed.—
Linford romance library
1. Love stories
2. Large type books
I. Title
823.9'2 [F]

ISBN 1-84395-569-5

Published by
F. A. Thorpe (Publishing)
Anstey, Leicestershire

Set by Words & Graphics Ltd.
Anstey, Leicestershire
Printed and bound in Great Britain by
T. J. International Ltd., Padstow, Cornwall

This book is printed on acid-free paper

1

Paula's new editor, Joe Saunders, tossed her the white, gilt-edged invitation to the ball.

'This is the only chance you'll get to see Beaumont Island while you're in Acacia Bay,' he said. 'It's been locked up like a fortress since the owner returned from the UK. Until a few months ago it was a popular tourist spot around these parts.'

Paula Bannister hadn't actually started with 'The Standard'. She'd called into the office to introduce herself as temporary replacement for her old friend, Maggie MacDougall, who was on three months' long-service leave. She turned the prestigious looking card over in her hand. It sounded rather like a society ball. As a reporter on a women's magazine based in Melbourne, she'd been hoping for something different while down here.

'I didn't bring anything to wear to a formal, Joe. I thought I'd escape the social set for a while.'

'You're staying at Maggie's place, aren't you? She'll have something in her wardrobe,' he said gruffly.

'You want me to go then?'

'Beaumont Powers is the tallest of poppies around here. When he invites us, we go.'

Paula smiled.

'That tall. Wow! I should do a profile piece on him.'

Joe put up his hand and shook his head.

'No fear. Don't approach him for anything personal. He hates journalists.'

She made a face as she cleared a chair and sat down.

'How come?'

'The Press gave him a hard time in England. His wife was killed in a car crash. They reckon she was leaving him at the time. She was a well-known socialite.'

Paula had been accused of having chronic curiosity by more than one person. Now she was very intrigued.

'Is that why you give him special treatment, Joe?'

Joe leaned back in his chair and crossed his arms.

'Your father may own this paper, but down here you play by my rules. This is a small, rural newspaper. We respect people's privacy. Keep your nose out of Powers' affairs. Go to the ball, show the flag, take a few notes and keep out of his way.'

'It sounds a bit dull.'

'Maybe, but you'll meet the volunteer community. By the way, what are you like with a camera?'

'I've earned some points for my photographs.'

'Good. Then take a camera and the invitation and scoot. I'm busy.'

Next morning, Paula consulted the office files on the important people of the district, to bone up on the man who chose to live on a locked-up island. He was a merchant banker, a widower with a daughter. His mother's family, the Beaumonts, had pioneered the small island. But what caught her breath was the pencilled reference in Maggie's familiar writing, 'Follow up the smuggling angle.'

So Beaumont Island had secrets. Her enthusiasm for the ball grew by the minute. Perhaps her two months in Acacia Bay were going to be really challenging.

'Joe,' she asked later, as casually as possible, 'there are some odd references about the island in the Beaumont profile. Anything I should know about before tonight?'

Joe didn't even look up.

'According to the gossips the place is haunted. And Maggie's mentioned smuggling.'

'Drugs? Could they be coming in from Tasmania?'

'Have you ever known a private island that didn't stir people's imagination?'

'I guess not,' she conceded, quietly turning what she had learned over in her mind.

As she prepared for the ball, her thoughts lingered over the widower with secrets. The newspaper file told her he was around forty. Nuggety, she mused, with receding hair, shrewd eyes, like most business men with their first billion behind them.

Pulling Maggie's electric blue taffeta with the flouncy sleeves over her head, she secured the zipper at the back and looked in the mirror, and groaned. It would have looked superb on her busty, bouncy friend, but on her it left much to be desired. Oh, well, life had its little setbacks, she said to herself as she pinned up her hair.

The phone rang as she reached for Maggie's evening purse.

'Will you be OK on your own tonight?' Joe asked.

'Fine. I'm looking forward to meeting the infamous Mr Powers.'

'Infamous? I've warned you Paula.'

'Have a little faith, Joe.'

She crossed her fingers. If there was a hint of a human-interest story surrounding Beaumont Powers, she'd quietly pursue it. Work on the women's magazine had grown repetitious and predictable. It was her big chance to prove to her father she could handle a daily newspaper job.

Paula felt tense, but excited, as she drove along unfamiliar, dark country roads towards the bridge which spanned the waters to Beaumont Island. At its edge, mist-hazed lights cast eerie shadows across its wooden structure. She eased off the accelerator and squinted into the blackness. But soon her headlights picked up a high cyclone fence barring the remainder of the bridge. Nearing it, she read the sign, in bold, luminous letters: 'Keep Out. Trespassers will be prosecuted' on the gate, which tonight stood open. A shiver ran up her spine as she drove through the opening and continued on until the red rear lights of a car ahead blinked in the darkness.

Finally her vehicle bumped off the bridge on to a ribbon of metal forming a rough roadway and she picked up other lights ahead. The darkness gave way to an avenue of gracious oaks, twinkling and swaying with tiny lights, sweeping up to the residence. Beaumont House loomed out of the mist, its grandeur stealing her breath.

Men with flashing torchlights directed her to the carpark, and as she stepped from her hatchback, a camera bag slung over one shoulder, her taffeta dress rustled in the light coastal breeze. She joined other guests making their way up the wide, marble steps of the mansion towards the splendid oak door which stood open, light and music spilling from it.

He was standing inside the magnificent reception hall backlit by bronze and crystal chandeliers. Coming in from the night, Paula blinked once, twice. She fingered uncertainly through her short cap of hair and blinked again.

Could this be Beaumont Powers? This tall, handsome man with dark hair which curled on to his brow and softened the lines and angles of his lean features.

As she advanced along the reception line, he turned frosty blue eyes upon her. They halted her momentarily. She forced herself to meet his cold stare, and smiled widely, as if she knew him from 'way back. There was no denying his imposing appearance, his tall frame. But those frosty blue eyes were something else!

'Paula Bannister of 'The Standard',' she said quietly.

'I don't believe we've met. Your invitation please?'

'Of course,' she muttered as she began rummaging through Maggie's wallet, though it was futile.

The invitation lay on her desk back at the office! It hadn't occurred to her to bring it. The media didn't need invitations to a do like this. Publicity was part of the event. Everyone knew that — except apparently this man!

Her fingers fumbled through the contents of her purse, and looking up, she saw that a glitter of impatience had replaced his icy stare. He was all but tapping his foot. What else could she do but own up?

'I apologise. I seem to have mislaid it and I've just transferred from Melbourne . . .'

She knew her excuse sounded lame and unprofessional.

Beau Powers wasn't amused. Not much more than a kid, he thought, with brown grey eyes, far too wide for her face. How could Joe Saunders have sent a new cadet reporter to his ball?

His fool-proof plans for tonight had really come unstuck. A knot tightened in his stomach. If only he'd cancelled the function when things started going wrong, instead of allowing sentiment to over-ride his judgment.

'Joe Saunders knows strangers aren't welcome on this island. You'll have to leave.'

As he spoke, she teetered on her unfamiliar high heels, lightly tilting forward into his arms. Hastily he put her at arms' length, swearing under his breath as he tried to ignore the warmth of her femininity. It wasn't unusual for women to make a play for him, but usually they were more mature women, women he had learned to handle. An audacious, young lady was something else. He was unsettled.

He watched her straighten her back, smooth out her dress and fix him with a steadfast gaze.

'A phone call to Joe would confirm my identity. Of course if you don't want the evening reported I'll leave immediately, though I can't see what harm a helpless woman can do.'

For once in his life Beau Powers felt cornered, and it annoyed him. He couldn't disappoint the Blind Foundation by banning a story and pictures in the local newspaper. As much as her presence concerned him, he had no option but to let her stay.

Turning to Lady Elizabeth Ferguson, the Foundation President, who stood beside him in the reception line, he smiled.

'Would you excuse me? I think the young lady and I should settle this privately.'

Taking Paula firmly by the arm he led her to one side.

'This conversation concerns only the two of us.'

Glancing around, he was reassured by the number of security people. They were positioned strategically, with instructions to report anyone who stepped outside the boundaries. And, of course, he'd personally keep her in sight to ensure she didn't talk to the staff.

'I haven't time to argue. You can stay. What did you say your name was?'

'Paula Bannister.'

'Then, Miss Bannister, let me see how good you are at obeying my rules.'

'Rules?'

'Find no excuse to go outside the

ballroom and reception area, or to talk to any of my staff, and you're responsible if your photographer takes more than six pictures.'

'But no-one takes only the number of pictures they'll use. We need a selection to choose from.'

'Tonight your photographer will have to make every shot count.'

'I'm taking the photographs myself, naturally, with your approval.'

She tilted her chin defiantly. He smiled briefly.

'If you're as good with a camera as you are with smart answers I'm sure you'll only need to take six.'

Her eyes shone.

'Shall we start with a photograph of you? We don't seem to have one on our files. Perhaps with Lady Elizabeth?'

Grudgingly he admired her spirit. She was the first person he hadn't been able to intimidate at will. It probably had something to do with her youth.

'Six photographs, Miss Bannister,

and that doesn't include one of me,' he replied.

Whatever happened, tonight had to be a pleasant, innocuous evening, though by the minute it was fast turning into a nightmare.

'I'll have you thrown out if you so much as try taking my picture. Now, you've pushed your luck far enough. So get on with the job. You're cluttering up the reception area.'

Paula turned aside, the temptation to call him a patronising so-and-so dangerously poised on her lips. He hated everyone from the media. His erratic behaviour confirmed it. But there was more. Beau Powers was deeply troubled by something. Sighing, she went in search of people and suitable locations for her pictures and background story, her eyes and her mind busy processing what she observed. Soon she was chatting and organising people for photographs. It was as well she could do it without much application, for her thoughts lingered on Beaumont Powers.

Paula had just finished photograph-ing Lady Elizabeth with her committee when she noticed Powers watching her intently in the background. The lights dimmed, the orchestra slipped into a modern waltz, and couples drifted on to the floor. He moved in her direction. Was he coming to ask her to dance? She shook herself, dismissing the fanciful notion, rejecting the disturbing thought which flashed into her head of being in his arms.

Hastily she turned her attention to her camera, wishing away her lively imagination. His only interest was in the number of frames she'd shot. In which case, he'd know she'd taken more than the mandatory six pictures. She shrugged.

'Here. I think you've earned it.'

Startled, she swung around to find a glass of white wine being placed into her free hand by a complete stranger.

'I'm David Medway. You're new in town, aren't you?'

'I'm filling in for Maggie MacDougall at 'The Standard'. The name is Paula Bannister.'

She held out her hand.

'Thanks for the drink,' she said putting the glass to her lips.

'My pleasure. Anything for a beautiful young woman in distress. I saw your awkward moment when you realised you'd no invitation with you.'

She smiled warmly.

'This really is the place for a grand affair, isn't it? Have you been on the island before?'

'Not since Powers returned from England. As an engineer, I've done a bit of work around, inspecting security installations, that kind of thing.'

'Tell me,' she said, curiosity driving her, 'why was the island suddenly closed to the public?'

He hunched his shoulders.

'Who knows?'

'How long has Powers been back?'

'Two, maybe three months. Why the interest? Planning an in-depth feature on him, are you?'

She smiled, her eyes ranging around the room.

'All this luxury, and a handsome, unattached squire thrown in — what girl wouldn't be interested? With your connections, David, I don't suppose you can suggest a way I can tour the island while I'm down here? Legally, of course.'

'Sorry.'

'What's the big mystery? Smuggling, ghosts?'

David grinned.

'He can't be hiding much. After all he has this huge crowd of people here,' she pointed out.

'And a legion of heavyweights protecting the property.'

Laughing, she caught sight of Powers, who stood on the perimeter of a group of people some distance away. He looked as restless as she felt, as he rocked on his heels and appraised the dancers circling the room. He stood in an ideal position from which she could take his picture. As David talked, her mind wrestled with the temptation to take it and worry later. The very worst he could do in front of his guests was order her out. Recklessly she turned to David.

'Dare me to take a picture of our host?'

'I wouldn't risk it, Paula.'

Ignoring what was clearly good advice, Paula fitted the tele-lens, and waited for exactly the right moment to trigger the motor.

Dance music, laughter and voices crowded the room. Still she waited, impatient. At last he looked her way. She prickled with heat and in one heart-stopping motion, her finger activated the camera button. The flash fired once, twice. She had captured Beau Powers' image on film.

Withdrawing the camera with shaky hands, she turned her attention to unscrewing the lens and placed the camera back into its case, expecting by the minute to feel a tap on her shoulder, a booming voice in her ear. She stole a look in her host's direction. He was in earnest conversation with one of the waiters. The sparkling chandeliers had masked the camera flash.

With the shot she had in her camera, a smart girl would leave now. She glanced across at Powers. His hawk-like gaze fell almost immediately upon her. She decided her best chance to disappear unnoticed would come at supper time.

'You've got your picture, but I bet you won't use it,' David's voice cut into her reverie.

'Probably not, unless I asked Powers' permission.'

She wondered why a strange look came over David's face.

'Permission for what?' a voice boomed, and Paula spun around.

Powers stood at her left elbow. So he knew about the photograph and had deliberately waited to tackle her! She took several breaths as she placed her camera bag on the vacant chair at her side.

'You startled me, Mr Powers. You know David?'

Her voice was a shade too bright. Paula Bannister prided herself on always being in control of her feelings in public, but in this man's presence, she felt disconcerted and uncertain.

'We've met in the course of duty,' he acknowledged coldly.

For awkward seconds there was silence, then both she and David rushed into conversation at the one time.

'I was just saying . . . '

'Are you happy with . . . '

Paula withdrew gratefully and David continued.

'The electric fencing on the vulnerable side of the island, are you satisfied with it?'

'You know about that?'

'I approved the permit.'

'The fence is to keep people off the place. That southerly side could be reached from the ocean by . . . er, by mutton bird poachers.'

Paula managed to prevent her mouth from flying open. Had he almost said smugglers?

'And drug smugglers?' she chipped in recklessly.

'Not in this part of the world. The island's a sanctuary for mutton birds,' he growled.

He fiddled with a cuff link. She'd hit a nerve. But soon he had her on the defensive.

'You need my permission to do what exactly?' he asked.

She started like a nervous deer and the colour of guilt rose in her cheeks. A manipulated version of the truth would have to do.

'Nothing really. I took more than six photographs. I kept shooting and quite lost count. I was saying to David a double page spread of pictures would look super if you agree.'

'I don't. Now, if you've finished your work, may I escort you to supper?'

'Excuse me?' she asked in amazement.

'Can I escort you to supper?'

She put her index finger to her cheek.

'Why do I have the feeling that over supper, you're going to insist on choosing the photographs and seeing the story before its printed?'

Powers actually smiled — a smile to melt even the most determined spirit. Paula excused herself for her weakness as he leaned closer, an unnerving, tingling whisper away.

'If I promise no shop talk will you accompany me?'

His scent, a warm, tangy mix of masculinity and fresh soap, hung in the air, sending her senses into a spin. Her will-power deserted her. With a rush of unbridled stirring in her body, a tremor of fear, she knew that in her lifetime she would never meet another man who would affect her so instantly and so dramatically.

2

Anxiety gnawed at Beau Powers' innards. Tonight two women had arrived on his island, uninvited. Either one could hijack his carefully laid plans.

His late wife's sister, Olivia, awaited him upstairs, but he seriously doubted her promise to remain there until the last of his guests had departed. Making a grand entrance to embarrass him was exactly the kind of thing she'd do. And, as if that wasn't enough, this unknown reporter was clearly up to something.

He'd observed her circling the crowd, getting along famously with people. He suspected her vivacity and those wide, innocent eyes could draw information from even the shyest person. It was imperative that she didn't find her way into the kitchen and engage the staff in conversation at supper time.

He tugged at a cuff link. Escorting her into supper seemed the best way of keeping her under surveillance in the dining-room. But she was hesitating about accepting his invitation. He moved closer.

'I'm all talked out about charities for tonight,' he said, pausing to press his memory for her name. 'You will rescue me, Paula?'

Colour flooded engagingly over her cheeks. It beguiled him that such a confident, impertinent young lady could blush.

'Well, Paula?'

He smiled down at her.

'Why, yes, it might be fun.'

She was blushing again. It was damned attractive, he thought; she was damned attractive.

As he'd watched her at work, he'd noticed little things. She walked like a young deer. Her short hair bounced engagingly over her forehead when she nodded and chatted to people. She was full of surprises, too. With laughter in her eyes, she thrust her arm through his.

'I'd love to rescue you, Mr Powers.'

Except for the orchestra which played gently in the background, everything else came to a sudden, cataclysmic halt. People turned disbelieving eyes upon them as they began to stroll towards the supper room. The silence and stares irritated him.

'You look a bit uneasy. Are you all right?' he asked Paula, looking down at her, feeling the warmth of her bare arm against the soft wool of his jacket.

'The women are watching with jaundiced looks. They're jealous.'

She smiled up at him before clinging harder to his arm, as if to refuel the annoyance of the onlookers. She didn't let situations throw her. He liked that, too. But he had no intention of relaxing or in any way trusting her.

'We've offended everyone except Lady Elizabeth and the Mayor. I arranged earlier for him to partner the President. Does it worry you?'

She tossed her head.

'Only that you were very confident I'd agree to be your partner. I dislike being taken for granted.'

She looked up at him, and then drew dark lashes down, once, twice over warm, brown eyes. His uncertain emotions about this intriguing young woman intensified.

As they entered the room, with its sparkling candelabra, cutlery, crystal flutes, and fine china, shimmering in the long table of beautifully polished mahogany, their reflections in the huge, gilt-edged mirror above the yellow-veined marble fireplace shone back at them. Though the dress Paula wore hung loosely over her small frame, she had obviously chosen it for its colour, for the vivid blue highlighted her eyes and enhanced her lightly tanned complexion.

Paula would have hooted with laughter at any suggestion that she was a day-dreamer, but here she was, without the slightest encouragement from him, hoping that tonight was just the beginning. Glancing about her, she wondered if someone hadn't sprinkled gold dust where she stood.

You're crazy, Paula, nothing will come of this brief encounter, she told herself. He hates reporters. And don't be misled by his invitation to accompany you to supper. It's his way of keeping an eye on you in the crowd. But reason was not enough to still her impetuous heart.

'Everything's so attractive, elegant, and the food smells wonderful,' she said nervously as she unlinked her arm from his and walked casually, she hoped, to the table.

'Hungry?' he asked.

Her heart skipped a beat. She looked into his extraordinary eyes before quickly returning her attention to the table.

'I think I'd like to try the scallops. Were they caught locally?'

He handed her a plate and served her a portion of the dish.

'Yes. In the ocean around these parts.'

As they moved from the laden table to a quiet corner of the room, Paula was mumbling to herself, 'This must have cost a fortune.'

Apparently he heard her.

'So you're interested in how much I've spent on tonight? I expect you'd like to quote the figure in your article.'

Had she mistaken the taunting tone of his voice?

'I hadn't thought about that. I meant my comment as a compliment.'

'You were prying.'

'You're mistaken, Mr Powers.' She smiled to ease the tension.

'I say you were prying. I never trust tabloid journalists.'

'I'm not a tabloid journalist. I work on a woman's magazine.'

She patted her mouth with a serviette, holding back her anger. He laughed quietly, cynically.

'All media people are the same.'

'I don't like your attitude, Mr

Powers. It smacks of prejudice.'

Paula took a sip from her drink, trying to cool down.

'We should close the subject before you get too heated. Can I fetch you some lobster?'

He began to move back to the table, confident he'd ended the discussion, but Paula was already thinking that her readers would love to know the cost of such a palatial affair. She caught up with him.

'Thank you, no. But may I ask one further question?'

She hurried on before he could interject.

'Everyone admires a generous benefactor, and in my experience, people who never get invited to these kinds of parties love to read the detail. But I suppose you're not going to tell me?'

He shook his head.

'Why don't you hazard a guess? That's what journalists do when the facts aren't available, isn't it?'

'Nonsense. Aren't there any journalists you trust?'

'None. They feed off people's misfortunes, slanting stories, always looking for the worst possible scenarios, hinting when the facts aren't available. They hunt in packs, yet have no tribal loyalty. Have you heard enough?'

Grim, scowling lines scored his features. Paula drew up her shoulders.

'I understand you've been deeply scarred by your experiences with the Press in England, but it doesn't give you the right to label and condemn all the media. Most journalists are fine, dedicated people.'

'You've only been around for twenty-four hours, yet you know about my clashes with the media in England?' he snapped.

'Who doesn't?' she bit back, amazed at the intensity of his anger.

'My point exactly. Yet it's none of your business.'

He raked a hand through his hair, and began speaking again.

29

'I agree there are times when the media has its uses. Tonight, for example. I want a feel-good piece in the paper, and I'll insist that I get it.'

He raised his broad shoulders, as if to challenge her to disagree. It was the arrogance of his body language which ruined her objectivity.

'Well, isn't that typical! You know I can't stop you. Joe will see you get exactly the story you want because in Acacia Bay you have influence. But do you have to rub my nose in it?'

'I wouldn't dream of it. It's too sticky for my taste, but very pretty,' he drawled, his equilibrium apparently restored.

Her finger was running over her nose before she realised it.

'I'm glad you approve, because I'm going to stick it one last time into your affairs. A question has been nagging at me all night.'

'Ask away. I can't, of course, guarantee to answer.'

'Wouldn't the Blind Foundation have

benefited more if you'd donated the cost of this evening directly to them?'

As she blundered through the words she recognised how intrusive it was to question the way in which the man chose to spend his own money.

'I mean, I would have thought the people here could afford to . . . '

Her voice petered out.

Reluctant to look directly at him, she straightened her shoulders and met his cold stare. Though her timing was out, her conviction that the Blind Foundation could have used the money more wisely, persisted. His quiet laugh chilled her.

'Aren't you going to share the joke?'

'Tonight is a special . . . ' he began then paused.

His eyes were cold with contempt. She waited, wishing she'd kept her mouth shut, willing herself to hold his gaze.

'Forget it,' he said eventually.

He'd left something unsaid. What was it? She had to know what those unspoken words were, so she pushed on at the risk of further alienating him.

'What do I call the function in the paper?'

'Ask your boss. He'll answer your questions from now on. And since you've finished your job, Miss Bannister, I suggest you leave quietly.'

A shiver ran up her spine at the tone of his voice.

'One of my men will escort you off the property.'

'I'll find my own way, thank you. Good-night, Mr Powers. Unfortunately, I can't say it's been a pleasure meeting you.'

A fitting exit, she reassured her flagging spirits, as she walked to the powder room with as much dignity as she could muster. The curious, questioning glances of people nearby followed. Her footsteps quickened.

At a basin she splashed cool water over her face, and was towelling it dry when a woman entered and smiled across at her in the mirrored wall.

'Hello. You've taken Maggie's place on 'The Standard' I hear.'

Dabbing at her face, Paula smiled briefly. She hoped the woman hadn't sought her out to get her name into the paper.

'Yes,' she said abruptly before softening her tone, for she had made enough bad impressions for one night. 'It's been a lovely evening, hasn't it?'

'Lovely. I'm Rosemary James, by the way, the pharmacist's wife. You must come and have coffee with me one day.'

Paula smiled.

'Thank you. I'd like that. Isn't this just a wonderful venue for a ball?'

'Mr Powers is very generous. His trust funds are legendary in these parts. Of course the Blind Foundation became his special concern after his daughter's accident.'

Paula went cold.

'Accident? You mean the one in which his wife died?'

'Yes, perhaps you didn't know. Little Claire lost her sight.'

'But it's returned now? His daughter can see, can't she?'

The hopeful words almost stuck in her parched throat.

'Claire only has shadowy vision, I understand. An awful tragedy for the child. To lose your mother and then . . . '

'And for the father, too,' Paula murmured as she dried her hands and hurried from the room.

'Give me a call once you've settled in. I'm in the book,' Rosemary James called to her departing figure.

Outside, a hefty-looking man awaited her.

'Miss Bannister,' he said, 'I have instructions to see you off the island.'

'I'm sure you have,' she said and brushed past him to the door.

Mist hung heavy in the cold, autumn air. She breathed deeply, wrapped her arms about her body, and waited for her eyes to adjust to the darkness. Behind her, her escort turned on a torch, lighting the way ahead.

'Good-night,' she said, trying to be courteous, when they arrived at her car.

With shaky fingers she opened the door and eased into the driving seat. At first try the engine refused to turn over. The man hovered, his presence mocking her. She took a deep, steadying breath and tried the key again. The car sprang into life. Thrusting the stick into gear, she pulled the vehicle on to the bitumen and drove back down the avenue.

It wasn't until she was turning the hatchback off the gravelled track on to the mainland road that she checked the seat for her camera. Her heart pounding, she jammed on the brakes. She'd left her camera in the ballroom!

3

Paula's sweaty hands slipped on the steering-wheel. As she swung the car around, and turned back to the island, a spray of stones flew from beneath her tyres. It was almost midnight when she put on her best smile and strolled up the steps of Beaumont Hall.

'I forgot my camera,' she told the men who guarded the entrance.

'The boss's expecting you, Miss Bannister,' one said, poker-faced.

She shivered, but under cover of the people leaving, she hoped she might be able to get into the ballroom, recover the camera and steal away before he found her. As she hurried to the chair where she had left her camera bag, she expected a heavy hand to fall on her shoulder at any minute. It didn't, and she understood why. The camera wasn't there.

She glanced about her. A waiter with a tray of empty glasses disappeared into what must be the kitchen, and she followed. One of the staff might know where Powers had put the camera and retrieve it for her.

'Excuse me,' she said approaching a plump, older woman who seemed to be in charge. 'I've misplaced my camera. You haven't seen it by any chance?'

As the woman turned to face her, Paula noticed the gentleness in her eyes.

'You must be the young reporter. Mr Powers is expecting you.'

Paula stifled a sigh of frustration. The prospects of recovering her camera and stealing away quietly were disappearing by the second.

'I wouldn't dream of troubling Mr Powers for something so trivial. Perhaps you could get it for me, please?'

'Mr Powers said you're to wait. He's busy seeing people off, but he shouldn't be long.'

'Actually I can't wait. My car's parked awkwardly and I'm holding people up. I thought I could run quickly inside and . . . ' Paula shrugged and smiled. 'You know how it is? Could you get it? I don't want to bother a busy person like Mr Powers.'

'Don't worry about your car, miss. The boys'll shift it if necessary.'

She patted Paula's arm.

'Why you're shivering, and you look pale. I'll make you a nice cup of tea. I'm Jessie Marks, the housekeeper, by the way. Now sit down.'

Paula had temporarily run out of ideas and spirit. She sank into a chair.

'That's sweet of you, Mrs Marks, but I don't want to be a nuisance.'

'Nonsense. Now don't worry about a thing. You'll have your camera back soon. I'll get that cup of tea. Milk and sugar?'

She bustled across to the bench.

'Weak black, please,' Paula responded, starting to wonder if getting off the island shouldn't be her first priority and worrying about the camera her second.

When Mrs Marks handed her a cup of tea, she wrapped her cold fingers about the cup.

'Thank you,' she said.

Mrs Marks stood at her side, as if on guard.

'Have you lived on the island long?' Paula asked to fill the silence.

'I've looked after the household since Mr Powers was a wee laddie.'

'Were you with him in England, Mrs Marks?'

'No. The island's my home. I looked after his mother until she died a few years back, and of course I'm in charge of the staff. I used to organise the tourist afternoon teas when people came out for the day.'

'So why did it close to visitors?'

Mrs Marks suddenly edged away.

'Please excuse me. I must get on with my work, miss.'

Paula reached for her arm.

'You've earned a rest. Sit down a while. Tell me about the family, the little girl? I felt just awful when I heard that she's . . . '

'Lost her sight?' a voice came from behind.

She turned sharply, almost spilling her cup of tea, and stared up at Beaumont Powers. In a knee-jerk reaction to her night of tension, Paula cried out, 'Mr Powers, why didn't you tell me your little girl's vision was affected in the accident? You let me go on . . . '

Her heart pounded against her rib cage.

'Making a fool of yourself? You did that all by yourself.'

'I'm so sorry. I was unpardonably rude.'

Beau's icy appraisal transferred to his housekeeper.

'Please excuse us, Mrs Marks. Miss Bannister and I must talk in private.'

Turning to Paula, he placed his hand around his wrist, and hissed, 'Come with me. Your camera's in my study.'

His fingers cut into her soft skin as

he almost tugged her into a long passageway.

'I should have sent you packing the minute you arrived without an invitation. You couldn't even be trusted to do something as simple as report on the ball and leave quietly. No, you have to start asking personal questions of everyone in your sights. I'm sick of it, do you hear?'

'The whole world can hear.'

She wrestled herself free, but kept pace with him as he strode the hallway.

Beau Powers was on an emotional tightrope, deeply troubled by something. His coldness was nothing more than a façade. Just now she'd discovered that beneath his remote indifference lay a formidable passion. Oddly enough it stirred Paula into action.

'You're being absurd. I'm not up to anything. Are you this suspicious of everyone you meet?'

He stopped, turned on her.

'Only those who think they have a right to dig around in other people's lives. Investigative reporting is the euphemism you use in your trade, I believe.'

He tipped his head mockingly, and stormed on. She couldn't deny she was intrigued, curious, but unethical?

'Don't lump me in with the odd nasty newspaper owners and reporters you've met. Mrs Marks and I were chatting about family things. Women do that, you know. I'm very sorry about your daughter, but I . . . '

'Leave Claire out of this.'

Paula longed to reach out and soothe the angry man in him, but knew any such attempt would be met by scorn.

'Beau, if you'd like to talk, I'm here for you.'

His eyes, magnificent, bedevilled, turned on her, and suddenly the crazy impulse to comfort and cradle him in her arms almost overwhelmed her.

'You think I'd talk to a reporter?'

'I'm a woman first.'

Despite his taunting reply, Beau Powers was tempted. He'd had no-one with whom he could share his grief. Claire was his only immediate family and his colleagues, staff and friends expected him to be strong. Yet, this brash, but engaging, young woman had somehow sensed his need. Or was she wearing a mask to lull him into a sense of security? He knew nothing about her. He hadn't felt so uncertain about anyone. He hadn't questioned himself or his motives in years. His fears about her returned to plague him.

'It isn't wise to pretend the problem doesn't exist. It won't go away. It needs to be confronted. Beau, if I can help somehow with . . . '

Lest the gentleness, which drifted into her voice, sway him, he spun away from her and hurried up the sweeping staircase. Whatever her hidden agenda, she confused him, and, damn it all, she aroused him. It had been a long time since he'd been with a woman. That had to be why this one was so utterly disturbing. He cursed under his breath at his frailty.

Storming blindly on, he took two steps at a time, anxious for the security of his study. She followed at his heels. Except for their footsteps and the echoes bouncing back at them from the high, flock-papered walls, they journeyed in silence.

Success and wealth had come comparatively easily to Beau Powers, while personal happiness eluded him. It had taken his wife's tragic death to free him from a marriage which should never have been, and with a fresh start in mind, he'd brought his daughter back to the beloved island of his birth. But soon that move had turned sour.

His mind recalled the memories as they passed through a network of silent passages. It wasn't until he stood at his study door and heard Paula, breathless, a yard or two behind, that his thoughts returned to his mission. He was weary. It had been a trying day, but he'd negotiated it unscathed thus far. Two more matters had to be attended to before he could finally breathe easily.

The first, to see Miss Bannister on her way. He removed a key from his pocket, and thrust it into the lock.

From deep within the house a clock chimed one. He heard Paula gasp as the sound echoed along the narrow corridors. He turned to her.

'Cinderella should have been home an hour ago,' she said, the suggestion of a smile on her lips.

'If it's any reassurance, the fairy godmother hasn't turned you back into Cinders. You're still wearing your ball gown, and its colour becomes you.'

It made no sense to compliment her, but her attempt to ease the tension between them, and the pallor of her usually glowing skin, warmed him. She looked feminine, vulnerable. How odd it was that someone as brash and streetwise as she could tug so forcefully on his emotions.

He strode into the room, switched on the desk light, bringing a soft glow to the room, and then pulled the heavy drapes around the casement windows.

45

Turning, he found Paula motionless in the entrance.

'Come in and close the door,' he commanded.

Paula inhaled deeply and took a few cautious steps, her glance all the while following his tall, lean outline as it cut through the muted lighting of the room — his room, with its musky sensual odour. Its forest-green Chesterfield suite, its heavy desk of mahogany, its shelves crowded with books, sporting trophies, newspapers scattered lazily at the clawed feet of a leather chair. She doubted if anyone would dare walk over its threshold without an invitation. But she had an invitation, so why hesitate?

'Come in. I'm not going to eat you,' he said gently.

As if mesmerised, she forced herself deeper into the room.

'I took the precaution of winding on the film and removing it from the camera.'

His gaze fixed on her, he removed the black and yellow film canister from his trouser pocket and held it aloft between thumb and index finger. Thankfully she quelled the impulse to grab the incriminating film. That would have aroused his suspicions. Instead, she smiled as she looked up at him, her head tilted provocatively.

'Beau,' she said huskily, 'please don't tease me. It's my first assignment and Joe will be so angry if I go home without the pictures.'

His top lip glistened with sweat.

'Come here, Paula,' he said, sweeping papers from the corner of his desk and propping on its edge.

'Excuse me?' She stumbled over the words.

'You heard. I asked you to come here.'

'It sounded like an order to me. Why should I?'

'Because I've got something you want.'

She moved an arm's length towards him and thrust out her hand.

'This is as close as I get. I want my

film, but don't expect me to beg.'

'As you wish.'

He dropped the cassette into her open palm and, as she closed her hand around it, his fingers snapped about her wrist, and he pulled her close. Tilting her face upwards, he said, 'You've been flirting with me, Miss Bannister.'

The warmth of his touch, the scent of him stirred her.

'Why would I flirt with you? It wasn't flirting. I was appealing to you.'

'You were flirting, Paula. Don't bother to deny it. You're so young but you're one most attractive woman and you scare me. Go home and forget you ever set foot on this island.'

How could she forget when in that brief interlude every sensitive nerve end in her body had tingled, when in that sweet intimate moment when he had touched her an unknown force of emotions had welled up inside her? Walk away? She couldn't do it. And his eyes, the way he looked at her, told her it wasn't what he wanted either.

Impetuously she traced her fingers along the silk lapels of his dinner jacket and whispered, 'I don't think you're scared of me. What frightens you are your feelings, and I'm not a kid. Do you know how old I am?'

He stood up.

'Older than I first thought, certainly, but at a guess nineteen or twenty, going on thirty.'

The pitch of her laugh was slightly hysterical.

'I'm twenty four. I'm an adult with all the feelings and emotions of a woman. Old enough to be kissed by a man with desire in his eyes. So why didn't you kiss me? You wanted to.'

He pushed roughly past her on his way to the back of his desk.

'Kiss an opportunist, like you? You won't compromise me that easily.'

He stood imperiously behind his desk.

'When you leave here I don't ever want to see you again.'

He seemed obsessed with the idea

that she had come to spy on him, and that every move she made was planned to that end. She moistened dry lips, dragged air into her hungry lungs.

'How dare you suggest I use feminine wiles to get my stories. I'm proud of the way I communicate with people.'

He stood tall, glared at her.

'Put words into people's mouths, you mean.'

'I'm tired of your cynicism, Mr Powers. I'm good at my job whether you choose to believe it or not.'

'Yeah, yeah. So why have you transferred from a successful magazine to a small regional newspaper?'

'I have my reasons,' she cut in, her heart quickening.

He dug his hands into the pockets of his trousers.

'Let me guess. You're running away from someone.'

'Wrong again,' she tossed her head. 'Now, may I have my camera and bag, please?'

He scowled as he retrieved it from a locked drawer.

'Take it and go,' he barked, thrusting the equipment in her direction.

'Thanks.'

She snatched it, avoiding his touch, and swung the bag angrily over her shoulder. In silence he pushed by her and opened the door. Once outside, he locked the room.

He was removing the key when Paula heard a door opposite open. Swinging around, she saw a woman step into the hall. Thirtyish, she wore a slinky white satin concoction. Black lustrous hair fell to her shoulders, heavy eyeliner widened her light eyes. Paula gaped unashamedly, her thoughts suddenly hijacked by the vision in white.

'So there you are, darling,' the woman purred before arching her eyebrows and sweeping Paula a wintry glance. 'I've kept out of the way of your guests, but you did promise to join me for a nightcap. I'm still waiting.'

Beau had described Paula as flirtatious, but this woman's performance left her back in drama school, Paula decided.

'Don't crowd me. Give me ten minutes to see Miss Bannister out.'

He turned back to Paula, his look thunderous.

'I'll show you to your car.'

She hurried to stay with him as he hurried towards the staircase.

Breathless, she gasped, 'If you're so anxious to get back to the vision in white I'll find my way out.'

'Not on your life. God knows where you'd poke your nose. You, Miss Bannister, get a personal escort off the island.'

'Poor Madame X, waiting so expectantly in her white negligée. She'll get very jealous and impatient, Beau, if you spend too much time with me.'

Paula hadn't meant to sound even remotely envious, but in truth she was. It hadn't once occurred to her that he might have someone special on the island. His laughter subsided, silence exaggerated their footsteps on the stairs. Her thoughts lingered with Madame X.

Curiosity finally compelled her to ask, 'Does she live on the island?'

'Who?'

'Madame X, of course.'

'Interested in her for a story, are you?'

The mockery in his voice was enough to really stoke the fires of indignation already burning inside her.

'I hadn't considered it. But, thanks for the tip. I can see the headline now, 'Love nest on Beaumont Island'. What do you think?'

Pausing, he glowered down at her.

'Try it and I'll have you sacked.'

'I don't think so. I dare you.'

'Don't tempt me.'

His tone was faintly teasing. Some of the coldness in his eyes melted. Perhaps he had decided it was the best way to handle her. But to her disappointment, he strode off, killing the conversation.

She called after him.

'You wouldn't succeed because my father owns the newspaper.'

'Well, now, that explains a lot.'

She quickened her step and was by his side when she announced brightly, 'Yes. So what are you going to do about that, may I ask?'

'Buy the paper if that's what it takes to get rid of you.'

'You'll have to buy a whole chain of them.'

He paused.

'Bannister? Bannister? Do I know the name?'

She suspected he was going to laugh openly, but he strode off. She caught him up again.

'In case you're wondering, you haven't any shares in Bannister Consolidated. My father owns it lock, stock and printing presses. One day it will be mine. Then I might be willing to listen to an offer.'

He swung back to her.

'You're a pain in the butt, Miss

Bannister Consolidated. It's time I turfed you out and returned to my assignation with Madame X.'

Suddenly, the sound of a chiming clock echoed through the stark, dimly-lit reception area. Two o'clock! She almost toppled over him, as she uttered a startled cry.

Glaring at his watch as if his look might influence the time, he growled, 'It can't be two o'clock! The whole place will be sealed off for the night.'

His fingers gripped her shoulders, stinging her flesh, and with a malevolent stare, he rasped, 'Why you, you . . . '

'Manners, Mr Powers, you're talking to a lady.'

'Ha! When I see Joe Saunders, I'll . . . '

'Strangle him?' she cut in again.

'With my bare hands.'

'Stop making a fuss and get your manager to escort me out, if you're so besotted by your lady love.'

'Do you have any idea how long it takes to secure this place? Of course you don't, or you wouldn't be asking me to wake up my property manager.'

'You padlock the place like a fortress. Goodness knows why.'

'To keep out people like you.'

'What makes you so twitchy when a reporter is around?'

She pushed her luck to the very edge.

'Is this my cue to say 'no comment'? With your lively imagination you should be writing fiction. You'd make a fortune.'

He turned then and headed for the ballroom. He gave the bell cord a furious tug. His bottom lip curled as he faced her.

'You'll have to stay the night. If I didn't know better I'd think you engineered this. Mrs Marks will show you to a room. And don't you dare move out of it.'

'Spend the night here? No way. I'll ask the manager to unchain the gate for me if you won't.'

Paula stalked towards the door. A few hours ago the opportunity to stay in Beaumont Hall had whet her appetite, but now that she knew its owner had a woman waiting for him she wanted to be gone from the place.

'Go for it,' he called to her.

She was halfway across the room when she spun around, her resolve gathering momentum.

'Count on it. I will.'

'Then there's a boat at your disposal if you don't mind wading out to it.'

'Pardon?'

'The autumn tides cut us off from the bridge for a couple of hours twice a day. One of them happens to be about now. Best of luck.'

With every ounce of pent-up anger she aimed her bag at his taunting features. It thudded against the door, its contents spilling around his feet. In one swift movement he gathered them up.

'Thanks for reminding me that I should relieve you of this stuff while you're on my island, especially these.'

He held up her ring of car and house keys before dropping them into his pocket. She flew across the room, ready to scratch out his eyes if necessary to retrieve her purse, but she was too late. He had securely tucked it under one arm and was closing the door in her face when she arrived.

'You so-and-so,' she railed.

He tilted his head in feigned apology and continued on his way.

'Heartless brute,' she shouted down the passageway.

The words echoed back to her, accompanied by mocking laughter.

4

Paula stood alone in the vast dining hall, fuming. Now what? She didn't have to wait long for her answer. Mrs Marks, a candlewick robe clutched about her ample middle, hurried into the ballroom.

'I've been instructed to show you one of the guest rooms, miss. You'll be quite comfortable. They have their own bathrooms and you'll find plenty of clean towels,' she said curtly.

'Thank you, Mrs Marks, but I'll stay in my car until the tide goes out and then leave,' she said firmly. 'I've got a rug. Now please, don't worry.'

'Do be sensible and use one of the guest rooms,' the woman interrupted anxiously.

'You go back to bed. I'll find my way out. I'm sorry you were disturbed.'

Mrs Marks sighed.

'If you change your mind, the guest rooms are upstairs along the gallery on your right. Ring the night bell at the back and someone will let you in.'

Silently Mrs Marks accompanied her to the door. The sound of the lock activating behind her caught at Paula's breath. She suddenly felt very lonely. It was eerily still, except for the distant sound of waves crashing against sand and the trees swaying in the wind. Her footsteps quickened as she hurried towards the carpark. On reaching the edge of the carpark she came to a halt. A vast, open field stretched in front of her. Her car was missing.

At the sound of footsteps behind her, she stifled a scream and turned to confront her pursuer. The powerful beam from a torch blinded her.

'Who are you? What do you want?' she choked.

'Sorry if I frightened you, miss. I'm Dan. The boss said to keep an eye out for you when you came lookin' for your car.'

'I don't frighten easily. Have you come to unpadlock the bridge gate?'

'My orders are to see you back into the house. Your car's locked away for the night so the salt air don't get to it.'

Numb with cold, she folded her arms across her body.

'How dare Mr Powers hold me here against my will. I'll have something to say about it, I promise you.'

'You'll have to take that up with the boss in the mornin', miss. My instructions are to accompany you back to the house. Now come along, miss, you must be freezing. The boss sent a cloak. I'll let you in through the back entrance, and you can go up the staff stairs.'

Surrendering, she accepted the soft garment from him and threw it about her shoulders, grateful for its warmth.

'Thanks, Dan,' she muttered.

'It weren't my idea, miss. You should thank the boss.'

Fat chance, she thought. Thanking Powers was the last thing she'd do. As she followed Dan back to the house, she sent mental daggers in the great man's direction. Dan unlocked a heavy side door and let her in.

'I think Mrs Marks told you where the guest room is. Good-night, miss. Sleep tight.'

'Good-night, and thank you again,' she said.

When the door swung closed, Paula shivered and huddled deeper into the mohair cloak. The gloom, the shadowy silence ate into her courage. On tip toe, she began climbing the staff staircase.

At the top, running off the right-hand passageway, she found a series of doors as Mrs Marks had mentioned earlier. She inched open the first one and peered inside. Her heart on hold, she entered, found it empty, and silently locked the door. As she placed her camera bag on a bedside table, she decided not to turn on the light, and by the unfolding daybreak, removed her dress and shoes. Next she set her wrist alarm for six o'clock, and finally slid beneath the warm duvet on the little bed, and fell into a restless sleep.

She woke to the shrilling and squabbling of seagulls on the shore below her bedroom window. Turning over, she swallowed. Her throat burned, her body ached, but, so graphic were the memories of last night, that she leaped from the bed. Her first priority was to get off the island, her second, to deliver the film to Joe.

Taking up two towels, which hung over a chair, she entered the adjoining door, before realising it wasn't the bathroom. The early-morning light revealed a much larger bedroom with heavy furnishings. Heart pumping, she hastily retraced her steps until a small, worried voice stopped her.

'Is that you, Miss Hines? Didn't you go to see your sister?'

Even in her fragile state, Paula recognised with growing interest that this was Beau's daughter, Claire. Commonsense told her to get out of there immediately, but she thought she may have frightened the child, so she hurried to the bed to reassure her.

'Don't be alarmed,' she said softly. 'You must be Claire. I'm Paula Bannister. I slept in the room next door overnight.'

She gently took up the child's hand to establish physical contact.

'You're a friend of my father's?'

'I'm a reporter on the local newspaper. I was late leaving the ball last night so your father suggested I stay over.'

Claire's voice found some colour.

'A reporter! Golly, you must be a real special friend. Daddy always says he hates reporters and won't have them near the place.'

Paula grimaced. What could she say?

'I only met him last night.'

'Then you're beautiful.'

Paula couldn't help laughing.

'No. My mouth's too wide, my curly hair looks a bit like a mop, and my eyes are boring brown. Oh, and if my voice sounds Hollywood husky, it's because I've got a rotten cold coming on.'

She guided the child's hand over her features. The delicate little fingers paused to run a second time through Paula's hair.

'I like your short hair. I wish I could get mine cut.'

'But it's beautiful — so long and black and glossy.'

Paula gently stroked the length of the child's tumbled tresses.

'I hate it, 'cos it gets tangly, but Daddy says girls should look feminine.'

'And you do. You're very pretty.'

A stage-managed cough cut into their conversation like a knife. Paula and Claire raised their heads together, as if caught in a conspiracy. Powers stood by the open door wearing a dark T-shirt and jeans, his black hair windswept. Paula gave a slight shudder as he advanced towards them.

'I see you two have introduced yourselves.'

Arctic blue eyes lanced into her. Suddenly she became conscious that under the towels draped lazily over her, she wore only filmy underwear. Her cheeks burning, she clutched the towels around her and jumped up.

'Excuse me,' she mumbled fleeing towards her room.

'Don't go, Paula,' Claire wailed. 'Tell her to stay, Daddy. We were just getting to know one another.'

'If I don't get to work, my editor will sack me. I'll come again soon, I promise,' Paula called hoarsely.

She was about to shut the door behind her when Beau's hand closed around its edge and forced it ajar.

'I'll talk to you after I've settled my daughter down. You have some explaining to do,' he hissed.

Her heart turning crazy somersaults, she scampered into her clothes, and confronted in the mirror by a pale, wide-eyed image, tried plumping up her hair to improve her appearance. As poorly as she felt, she prepared herself for his entrance.

He arrived in a few imperious strides, and with studied silence closed the door. When he turned cold eyes upon her, she held her head high.

'What were you doing in my daughter's room?'

'I didn't know it was her room. I thought it was the bathroom.'

'There is no bathroom in this room.'

'Mrs Marks said all the guest rooms had bathrooms.'

'This is not the guest wing.'

'But she said the rooms on the right at the top of . . . '

She put her hand to her mouth.

'I see what's happened. She meant the front staircase. I came up the back. You can't mean I slipped past your surveillance cameras,' she added in a mocking tone.

'I knew what room you came into. I set a guard up outside. But I didn't count on you waking so early and finding your way into Claire's room. I underestimated your cunning again.'

Paula whispered painfully, her chin defiant.

'It was an honest mistake.'

'Honest? When you realised you were in Claire's room why didn't you leave? You knew I wouldn't approve.'

'I thought I might have scared her. I needed to explain.'

She broke into a fit of coughing.

'Get something on, woman. You're half-naked in that dress.'

He wrenched the mohair cloak from the bed post and flung it in her direction. It fell at her feet. With two quick paces he retrieved it and draped it carelessly over her shoulders. She drew it around her with trembling fingers.

'How can you think I sought out your daughter, after the fuss you've made about your privacy?'

'I want you off the island now.'

'As soon as you return my purse and my car.'

'The purse is on the hall stand. You'll find your car waiting at the entrance. Goodbye, Miss Bannister.'

As Paula broke into a coughing fit she fell back on to the bed, afraid she might pass out. Claire burst into the room.

'Daddy, is Paula sick?'

In the twilight between consciousness and unconsciousness, she heard his voice soften miraculously.

'No, possum. Go back to bed until Mrs Marks comes up to dress you.'

Paula wasn't sure what happened after that, but the next thing she knew for certain was she was alone, tucked into the bed wearing a cosy nightgown. She glanced at her wrist watch. Heavens, it was after ten o'clock. She had to get to the office with her film. Snuffling, she swung her legs out of bed, and stumbled across to her dress. She was coughing again.

At the sound of the door opening, Paula struggled back to bed as quickly as her spongy legs would carry her. Beau stood there. She pulled the sheet to her chin trying to hide the colour which swept across her cheeks.

'I have to get away,' she heard a

distant voice whisper, and was aston-
ished to find it was her own.

'You should have thought of that last
night.'

'My camera, my pictures, I have
to . . . '

'I've seen to all that. They've been
delivered to your editor with a
message that you won't get to the
office today.'

In a temporary moment of lucidity,
she recalled the forbidden shot of Beau
Powers on the film. Abruptly she sat
upright.

'You sent the undeveloped film, too?'

'Naturally.'

Paula took a long breath, gathering
her nightgown around her. She was hot,
cold, aching. She fell back on to the
pillows.

'Tired?' a distant voice asked.

As if in a dream, she watched him
move to the bedside, ease himself on to
it, place his hand to her head.

'You're running a fever. Dr West will
be here shortly. Now go back to sleep.'

Wearily she turned away. The under-sheet, the duvet were resettled about her shoulders, by that same cool hand. As she drifted off to sleep she thought someone with a rich, cultured voice growled, 'You're doing what you're told. There has to be a first time for everything.'

Dr West pronounced she had a virus and would have to stay in bed for several days. Beau dug his hands into his pockets.

'It's not convenient, West, especially if she needs medical help and nursing.'

He punched out the words, confirming he would brook no argument.

'But, Daddy, Paula's too sick to go home and Miss Hines won't be back for a while,' Claire said anxiously.

The child then turned her eyes to Paula.

'Paula, I can look after you.'

'She can't be moved for at least a few days, Powers,' Dr West said and snapped his black case closed.

'Frank, I can't risk her giving Claire an infection.'

'The child's not in any danger. The infectious period's over. Keep her away for a day or two to be on the safe side.'

'I want to go home,' Paula said in a hoarse whisper.

'In a few days, Miss Bannister.'

Beau and Claire departed with Dr West, but minutes later Beau returned.

'In case you think of going for a midnight stroll, or anything equally as stupid, I remind you, the rest of the house is out of bounds.'

'I expect you have a guard at the door anyway,' she said.

'I expect you're right.'

He swung on his heel and Paula fell into a dreamless sleep.

For two days, Paula drifted in and out of sleep. Her only visitor was Mrs Marks, who brought her meals and monitored her medication, but refused to be drawn into any conversation.

On the third day, Claire was allowed to visit in the afternoon for an hour, and on the fourth day, she spent most of the afternoon by Paula's side, obviously hungry for company.

'It must be really cool living on a little island like this one,' Paula suggested.

'I suppose, but I hardly ever see anyone.'

'I bet you and your father do some great exploring.'

Paula indulged her curiosity about everyday life on the island.

'He's very important. I wish people didn't need his advice all the time so we could do more things together. Once I had a little dog, but it was too hard for me to know where he was. Paula are you listening?'

'I was thinking how lovely your hair is. When the sunshine catches it, it glows like satin.'

'Oh, pooh, who cares? It gets knotty.'

'Then we shall ask your daddy if you can come across to the mainland and have it cut after I go home. Afterwards we could have a picnic.'

Claire's voice rose excitedly.

'Could we have it on my birthday?'

Paula groaned inwardly. Why had she made a promise she wouldn't be permitted to keep?

'Is your birthday soon?'

'In two weeks, I'll be eleven.'

'Eleven? Your dad would have to agree to the picnic first.'

'And my hair cut. Aunty Olivia thinks my hair's too long.'

'Your aunt's here? That's nice for you.'

Madame X? Paula's heart quickened. Claire shook her head.

'She's snotty. She expects everyone to fuss around her. She's mummy's sister.'

So the glamorous Olivia was Beau's sister-in-law! Was that all she was to him? Paula's mind took crazy, irrational twists and turns. She rubbed her temple, and was relieved shortly afterwards when Mrs Marks arrived to take the child off for her bath. Alone, she tried to unravel the riddle of the island

though her thought processes sometimes became hopelessly tangled. She
hadn't seen Beau once since she'd been
confined to bed four days ago. But
when he learned Claire had spent most
of the day with her, tonight she
expected him to storm into her room.

The evening dragged on. Beau didn't
come. It was late when she crawled into
bed, weak and tearful, and closed her
eyes to blank out the images swirling
through her mind — haunting images
of a man with secrets who couldn't
come to grips with his daughter's
disability; of a lonely child wandering
uncertainly through a mansion inhab-
ited only by adults.

Claire spent much of the fifth day
with her.

That night, sitting by the bed, waves
of loneliness swept over Paula. For the
first time in years she missed having a
family. She missed Claire, but what was
even more disturbing, she yearned to
see Beau. Glancing into the vanity
mirror, she groaned. A mass of tumbled

hair, eyes too wide for her pale face, and a pink nose stared back at her. The brush fell from her hand when a tap sounded on the door.

'It's Powers. Are you receiving visitors?'

Her pulse quickening, she pulled the bathrobe tightly about her, flattening her hair, dabbed at her nose. Half excited? Half afraid?

'Come in, if you have the guard's permission,' she said lightly.

When he stepped into the room, his masculine beauty stole her breath. In dark business clothes, Beau Powers looked every inch the handsome, executive multi-millionaire. But her ready smile froze on her lips when she looked into icy blue eyes which held only contempt.

'No guards. You're free to leave. Shall we say tomorrow morning?'

'Afraid I might start wandering around and discover something?' she snapped, overcome by disappointment.

Tears prickled behind her eyes. She

dragged her lashes over them, holding back the flow, determined not to reveal how much his callousness had hurt.

'Back to your old, impertinent self, I see. That's a sure sign you've recovered. You have a job to go to, don't you?'

'So you still see me as a threat?'

She fingered a single tear as it trickled down her hot cheek.

'You're crying? The brash young reporter reduced to tears?'

Amused incredulity warmed his glance. 'I am not,' she choked, the sudden shift in his attitude the catalyst for a shower of tears.

She turned away, though they were beyond hiding.

Beau hadn't seen a woman cry in a long time. When his wife was hurt, she used to laugh coldly and pour scorn on him, and Olivia had the same hard, brittle edge. Countless times he thought he might be wrong about Paula. There was a softness, a gentleness about her. It shone sometimes in those wide grey eyes; the curve of her mouth. He hurried to her side, offered her a crisp white handkerchief. She pushed it aside.

'I'm not crying.'

He felt awkward, uncertain. He eased himself on to the bed, tilted her chin with his hand, and looked into her shimmering eyes. With the pad of his finger he captured a tear and held it up.

'Then what's this? You're crying, Paula. Why?'

She shook her head.

'I'm still a bit fragile, I suppose.'

There were dark smudges under her eyes. Her skin was pale. She couldn't have feigned her illness, or the fact that it had tested her strength, yet she had not lost her spirit.

'I've been rough on you, but you have to understand that I've got a lot on my mind and I can't have you here any longer,' he began awkwardly, careful not to give too much away.

'I'm used to male bullies,' she cut in.

'Attracted to us are you?'

He grinned.

She nodded, smiling uncertainly.

'Yes, my father's one.'

'Paul Bannister? He sounds like a top guy. Frank West told me he got his start in journalism down here as a sixteen year old. Built up his empire in a very short time.'

'That's Dad. Admired by all for his success. I was ten when my mother died. He dealt with it by building himself a newspaper chain. I hardly ever saw him.'

'It's tough out there in the business world, young lady. Success doesn't come easily. When you're older you'll understand your father better.'

She sighed, dabbing at the last of her tears with a tissue.

'Talking to you is like talking to the wall of a squash court. You bounce everything back at me. I forgive my father week in, week out for putting his work ahead of everything else, including me, because I love him. But sometimes it needles me. And will you stop calling me young lady in that paternal way? I told you, I'm twenty four.'

He'd quite forgotten it. At the moment she looked young and vulnerable with her pale skin, pink nose and tangle of curls. He studied her closely.

He was suddenly conscious their knees were almost touching as they sat opposite one another. He ran the tip of his tongue along dry lips.

'Have you any idea how much older I am than you?'

'Yes, but it's not important to me.'

As she gazed up at him he was bewitched by her fragile beauty, the tenderness in her grey eyes, and he knew he wanted her as he had wanted no other woman. Every fibre of his being entreated him to seize the moment, to gather her in his arms. But he couldn't get sidetracked by his feelings. A slip-up here and he could lose everything precious to him. He moved to one side of the bed, breathed deeply.

'Age has nothing to do with how I

feel, you know,' Paula said.

Gently he cradled her hands into his. They were soft, feminine, yielding.

'Paula, you're feeling fragile, vulnerable because of your illness. I'm almost forty.'

'Forty is beautiful. I love forty,' she whispered, clinging tightly to his hands.

He touched her lips with the pad of one finger.

'It does matter. You can't waste your youth on me. I'll hurt you again and again. You've got the world in front of you. Go out and tame it.'

She paled, looking impossibly vulnerable. He had to get away before he gave way to his heart's urge.

Brushing his lips to her forehead, he said, 'I won't see you again, but if you're not up to leaving in the morning, tell Mrs Marks.'

His gaze shifted restlessly over her before he forced himself towards the door. There he hesitated and turned back to look at her one more time.

'Have a wonderful life, beautiful lady,' he said.

5

If she doubted it before, Paula knew now this man had stolen her heart. She couldn't have a beautiful life without him. And the way he looked at her told her he loved her. She couldn't let him walk away.

'Please don't go,' she cried. 'Why are you so terribly afraid of falling in love?'

'I told you once you scare me. You're a tantalising breath of spring, but, Paula, the time's not right for us. I can't afford to get diverted. I've got too much going on at the moment.'

'Nothing is more important than two people loving one another. I love you and I think you love me,' she murmured, putting out her arms. 'Come back to me, Beau.'

'Don't do this, Paula.' He laughed harshly. 'You're confusing desire with love. I don't love you. I want you, but you're in my way.'

His mouth tightened into a hard line.

'In your way?' she gasped.

They were not the words of the man who just now had gazed at her with heated passion. Could he be right? Had her illness affected her thinking?

'Very well, I'll leave tomorrow,' she said on a shallow breath.

'Try to understand. You're beautiful, you attract me and you have from the beginning.' He gestured with his hands. 'But I'm not going to take advantage of you when there's no future in the relationship.'

She'd stopped thinking clearly, was close to tears.

'Why would you want me when you've got Aunt Olivia dispensing her pleasures at the moment?'

He pounded a fist into his other hand, and Paula jumped.

'I don't believe this. You've been pumping Claire about Olivia, haven't you? Fool me for trusting you alone with my daughter. You're so clever, so manipulative. For two pins I'd . . . '

Paula flinched as if she'd been struck.

'Do what you like,' she said, despondent, knowing he couldn't hurt her any more than he had.

'I expect you out of here after breakfast tomorrow morning. Heaven only knows how much you've used Claire to delve into my affairs. If you breathe a word of anything she's told you, print a word . . . '

She cut in.

'The only thing I've learned from your daughter is that she's desperately lonely, isolated out here in a household full of adults, or hadn't you noticed?'

'My daughter is safe here.'

'From whom for goodness' sake?' she blazed.

'From the likes of you and your meddling colleagues.'

She stared back at him, unable to fathom the depth of his anger. He spun on his heel and left, slamming the door. It was over, and she had lost.

Next morning, Paula glanced in the

mirror. She looked as poorly as she felt, but she was resolute. She would not leave without saying goodbye to Claire. With Mrs Marks at her heels, she knocked and entered the girl's room.

'Sunshine, I'm off this morning,' she said, taking Claire's hand.

'You're cold, Paula. Is it 'cos you and Daddy were fighting last night? I could hear you.'

Paula dragged in air.

'I'm sorry if we sounded as if we were arguing.'

'I wasn't listening, honest, but I hear better than other kids. Anyway, I curled up under the covers when your voices got loud. That's what I used to do when Mummy and Daddy quarrelled. I hated it.'

'We had a difference of opinion, nothing we can't patch up in a day or two.' Paula crossed her fingers. 'And it's not why I'm going home. I'm better now. But I hate leaving you. We've had fun, haven't we?'

'I haven't asked Daddy about getting

my hair cut, or having a picnic for my birthday yet. He's been a real grouch lately. But I will.'

Paula smiled.

'What a wise, little thing you are,' she said placing her arm about Claire's shoulders.

'I hope Daddy says yes to the picnic. Now Aunty Olivia's gone he might be happier.'

'Has she?' Paula slipped out.

It was churlish, but it pleased her to think that Beau had lost his companion. Could that be why he seemed to turn to her last night? Suddenly she was besieged by self-doubt. Why would someone like Beau love her? Inexperienced, too young, unsophisticated. She was all of these. And if that wasn't enough, he'd crushed her by saying she was in his way.

Claire tugged at her arm. This would be the last time she'd see Claire, unless she could persuade Beau to change his mind. She'd try in a day or two after things cooled down.

When Paula returned to work, a copy of 'The Standard' in which her pictures of the ball had appeared lay on her desk. She turned the front cover and found six of her photographs on page three. Joe, who was passing, nodded.

'You take a mean picture, Paula. The page looks good.'

'It would have been better as a double-spread. So many people had to be left out. It's disappointing for them. And by the way, don't ask me ever to set foot on Beaumont Island again.'

'Didn't I warn you to keep your nose clean?'

'I'm not Powers' flavour of the month, am I?'

Paula tilted her chin, afraid to ask what the great man had said about her.

'Yet he allowed you to take those pictures of him. You must have made an impression.'

She drew in her breath. The pictures, the ones she'd taken in a moment of recklessness! Joe had noticed them on the contact sheet.

'You mentioned them to him?'

'Should I have?'

'No. Like lots of things that night, the pictures just happened.'

'You mean there's more?'

'Surely Powers listed all my indiscretions?'

Joe narrowed his eyes over the top of his glasses.

'He certainly criticised me for sending a newcomer because it put you at a disadvantage.'

'He said that?'

She frowned, wondering why Beau hadn't presented a catalogue of complaints about her.

'Is there something you're not telling me? What did you get up to?'

'Don't tell me that island is secured as tightly as a nuclear waste depot just to keep out journalists, Joe. There's more to it. Maggie could be right about smuggling.'

'Rubbish. Have you thought Powers' intention in banning visitors might simply be to protect his daughter from gossip and sightseers?'

'I have this odd feeling that he's waiting for something really big to happen.'

Joe raised his shoulders.

'You've been reading too many stories. Think about it. The poor blighter's lost his wife, his kid's nearly blind, and those wretched English tabloids lived on his doorstep for weeks, creating ugly rumours. How would you feel?'

No different, she thought, dispirited. She longed to help him, but he rejected her. Inside, it hurt. On the outside it was hard to pretend.

As Paula tried to refocus on her work, her attention returned to Claire, and her promise to take the child on a picnic for her birthday. She'd put off asking Beau's permission too long. Tomorrow, she resolved.

The next day, the contact sheet of her island photographs lay on her desk waiting to be filed. She left it there, silently repeating over and over, 'I don't want to see Beau's picture.'

But the sheet drew her irresistibly, and soon she was running her magnifying eye-piece over it. She'd caught a lonely, far-away expression in his extraordinary blue eyes, as if he were wandering alone by the cold, deserted shores of his island. She felt a swift, involuntary tug at her heart, quickly followed by a flicker of guilt. What if Beau found out about the forbidden photo?

Could she destroy the evidence of her impetuousness? Not without bringing on a major enquiry. The people in the other pictures would want to order prints. Sighing, she clipped the sheet into the binder, asking herself why she was letting him get to her. Where was her pride? He didn't want her. He was messing up her life, jack-booting his way over all the certainties she had in place about herself and her feelings.

The phone on her desk rang, interrupting her thoughts. She seized it up and snapped into the mouthpiece.

'Paula Bannister. Yes?'

'If I've caught you at a bad time . . . '

The rich timbre of Beau's voice came to her, pumping her heart.

'No, it's all right. I'm always edgy at deadline time,' she muttered.

'I was hoping you might get away for coffee. I'm in town now, but if you're too busy, perhaps some other time?'

Paula's heart did a triple somersault before it settled into a racy overture. Had she heard correctly? He was suggesting they meet for coffee! Well, it would give her an opportunity to talk to him about Claire.

'For coffee?' she repeated. 'I'm afraid I couldn't get away.'

She intended to say until four thirty, when the paper would be safely locked into printing, but Beau broke in.

'I understand. It's Claire's birthday on Saturday. You suggested a picnic to her. I'd like you to honour that promise.'

'I'll be glad to, but I thought . . . '

'We'll pick you up at your cottage.

Shall we say eleven o'clock? Mrs Marks will pack a picnic basket.'

Paula sat staring at the phone for seconds after he hung up, unable to comprehend what had happened. You're a fool, she told herself. He'll go on hurting you because you don't have the capacity to hide your feelings or run from them. But she'd promised Claire, and she couldn't let the child down.

On Saturday morning, Paula lifted the curtains and looked out upon a world shrouded in mist. A stormy day ahead in more ways than one, she thought, dreading the next few hours. But when the bell finally sounded, an uprush of expectation scorched through her body. Adrenalin pumping, she hurried to the door.

Beau was wearing a white T-shirt under a dark leather jacket, the collar turned up against the cold. She blushed as she looked up at him. Would he always send her heart into overdrive? She forced a smile.

'Good morning, Beau, how are you

and Claire? We've chosen a rotten day for a picnic, haven't we?'

His glance raked over her. She bristled at its cold indifference. He could at least try to be pleasant for Claire's sake.

'Get yourself a warm coat. There's a southerly blowing off the Strait.'

Impetuously, she clutched his arm.

'Beau, this isn't going to work unless you make a giant effort to be pleasant. We'll never be able to fool her that all is well between us. She's much too perceptive.'

His hand felt harsh and taut as he brushed her off.

'I gave my Oscar a shine before we left. I'll do whatever's required to make the day happy and I know how skilful you are at acting. Let's get the show on the road.'

She ignored his sarcasm, her concern now centred on Claire. She turned away to fetch her coat, her emotions catching up with her, afraid she might do something foolish like reach out to him; afraid the tell-tale moisture gathering in her eyes would betray her.

He was leaning against the door jamb, his dark hair, disturbed by the breeze, his hands pocketed, looking out upon her garden when she returned. She had thrown a woollen duffle jacket over her arm and carried a light cloth bag over one shoulder. Again her heart did a flip. Why couldn't he be hers? Why did he want her out of his life?

'Did you remember to polish your Oscar?' he asked quietly.

Her attempt at a laugh failed.

'So the pretence starts now,' she said.

'Now.'

He held her jacket while she shrugged into it, and then took her arm. As their bodies drew together, Paula almost recoiled from the fire of the collision, and involuntarily tensed every muscle to stem the shock waves. How could she get through the day? She'd do it for Claire.

'Paula, Daddy's packed the guitar, and Mrs Marks has made us chicken and salad, and a cake,' Claire called from the open window of the car as they approached.

Paula laughed gently. She felt better already.

'How's my birthday girl?'

'Next to me, Paula.'

Claire's hand patted the leather, as she wiggled her bottom into the centre of the bench seat.

'Here, hold my bag. I have a present for you, but you can't open it until later.'

'Please, pretty please, let me have it now.' The youngster chortled.

Paula hugged her.

'Later, when we cut your birthday cake.'

'This is the first time I've been off the island for a really long time.'

'But you love the island, darling,' Beau said.

'You say you love it best after you've been away, Daddy. Me, too.'

No-one could have guessed the strain Paula was under as she took Claire's hand into hers and resolved quietly to make the day as wonderful for the child as possible.

'I'm taking you to visit Seal Island,' Beau announced. 'Have you been there yet, Paula?'

'I've only read about it in the tourist brochures. It sounds fascinating.'

The road twisted and turned through grazing land, every now and then coming so close to the ocean that Paula was breathless with its majesty and moods. She described every scene to Claire.

When Beau pulled the estate car into a barren, windswept bluff high above the ocean, Seal Island was almost hidden by driving rain and sea spray. As he alighted from the car the rain tumbled down, as if outraged by their arrival and, his arms wrapped about his body, he hastened back into the car.

'Now what? We can't do anything in this weather.'

'Why not come back to my place?' Paula said. 'We can have our lunch there. We'll spread out the rug by the fire, like a real picnic.'

Claire managed a smile. 'I suppose so,' she said.

After three o'clock, Beau was tidying the remains of the lunch, while in the kitchen Paula inserted five sparklers into the birthday cake Mrs Marks had sent, lit them, and carried it into the room. Claire clapped her hands.

'I can hear a fizzing sound, and see a little glow. I know they're not candles.'

'They're sparklers.'

Claire clapped her hands again. After Beau helped her plunge a knife into the cake they joined hands and sang a lively 'Happy Birthday'.

'Now you can open your present,' Paula said, more relaxed than she'd been all day, placing it in Claire's hand.

The child peeled off the wrapping paper and prised open the little velvet box with eager hands.

'It's a bracelet,' she gasped. 'A charm bracelet! I can feel a horseshoe and a

key and a four-leafed clover, and a
. . . kangaroo.'

Beau stood by, grim, his annoyance
at her gift obvious, sending Paula into a
hasty explanation.

'My mother gave it to me on my
eleventh birthday. It's too small for me
now, so I want you to have it. There's
room for more charms. Ask Daddy to
put it on your wrist.'

'My bestest yet present. Thank you,
Paula.'

She held out her wrist and Beau
fastened the bracelet around it.

'Paula has been far too generous,' he
said gruffly.

'Would you like me to read 'Anne of
Green Gables'?' Paula hurried on,
anxious to take the spotlight from her
gift.

Claire nodded as she stretched out
her arm and dangled her bracelet.
Pleasure ribboned through Paula at the
child's delight with her gift, and
spontaneously she asked Beau to take a
picture of them as a memento of his

daughter's birthday party. Soon he had both girls laughing as he made funny noises and faces at them and triggered the camera. And then they settled on the sofa and Paula began reading. As she turned the pages of the book, Claire's eye lids drooped, her head fell across Paula's arm.

'We should get you to bed, young lady,' she said.

Beau eased his child from her arm to his own.

'We're just like a family, aren't we, Daddy?' Claire murmured.

'Yes, possum. Have you had a happy day?'

As he spoke, he buried his gaze in the fire's dancing flames. Was he thinking of his wife and their life in England? Claire fell asleep, and Paula suggested Beau put her to sleep in her spare room. He hesitated.

'I'd rather she was out here where I can keep an eye on her. If she wakes in a strange house . . . '

'We can leave the doors open. You'll

hear her if she's upset,' Paula said, wondering if, like her, if he was a little afraid to be alone with her, or did he have another reason for wanting to keep his daughter within sight?

'If you're sure we'll hear her.'

He shrugged and Paula led the way to the bedroom, where Beau settled his daughter between the sheets and drew up the blanket. She loved the gentleness with which this powerful, sometimes intimidating man, pushed aside Claire's dark hair and kissed her forehead. If only she could arouse that kind of tenderness in him.

The child stirred and mumbled, 'I love Paula, Daddy, don't you?'

'Go back to sleep, possum,' he whispered.

Paula heard him deny the question with a sinking heart, and hurried back to the sitting-room, where an awkward silence fell between them. They were alone, and she was uncertain. He threw a couple of logs on the fire.

'The rain's cleared, but I think we're

in for a chilly night,' he said.

'I'll put on coffee.'

Paula retreated to the kitchen to regain some composure. When she arrived with the coffee, he stretched his legs, eased more comfortably into the folds of the sofa. These would be the last precious hours he'd spend with her. He had to say goodbye tonight and mean it.

She settled on the rug, tucking her feet beneath her. She had her back to him, yet every fibre of his being registered her presence. He could hear her shallow breathing, see how the muted light caught the lighter shades in her hair so that she appeared to have a halo. What an absurd idea. Paula was no angel! He smiled. He knew so little and yet so much about her.

Silent seconds ticked by. The room had grown hot, too hot. Restless, he rose from the sofa, felt her glance follow his movements.

'Paula,' he began slowly, and then pushed on quickly, 'we can't see one another again. You do understand that? This has to be it. No more contact. No more promises to Claire.'

'You can't still think I'm a risk to your privacy. Surely I've proved I wouldn't do anything to harm you or Claire.'

'It's not that simple.'

He shrugged. He didn't have any satisfactory answers. He returned to the fireside, and eased himself down on to the carpet to sit beside her, initially to soften his words. But being so close to her was a mistake. He yearned to take her in his arms. She was so lovely. He ought to move, yet he couldn't. He almost forgot everything else, even what he was saying. He couldn't let his defence down now.

'I want to trust you, Paula, God knows I want to trust you. I've never wanted anything so much in my life, but I can't risk it,' he began.

She faced him and laughed bitterly.

'Because I write for a women's magazine? I can't believe that.'

'You're a journalist — one who's shown too much interest in the island.'

'All I want is to understand why you've rejected me. I know it has something to do with the island being locked up. I'm not after a journalism award. I need answers. I've fallen in love with you and I'm not giving up on you without a fight.'

Her honesty had him almost caving in. He stiffened his resolve.

'Even though I've asked you to respect my privacy?'

'I'd never betray your trust. I just need to know the truth.'

Her wide eyes, the feel of her hand on his arm, all filtered deep into his being. How could he not confide in her? Yet still he denied her.

'My secret is so confidential, so serious, I daren't risk it.'

'How can I convince you your secret is safe with me?'

He'd hurt her so much already, and he loved her. There, he'd finally admitted it to himself, he loved her. He looked down at her, lifted her hand into his, and taking the biggest chance of his life, said quietly, 'I don't want to go on hurting you. If I tell you, will you promise never to breathe a word of it to another soul?'

6

Beau felt Paula's hand tighten about his. He heard her draw in her breath, then she whispered, 'I don't think I want to understand any more. It sounds so final, so threatening.'

'It is, and I'm asking you to forget about us.'

He looked down at her lovely face, the gentleness in her gaze, and knew he could safely tell her what only a handful of trusted friends knew.

'But would knowing end any hope of us ever being together? I don't think I could bear that.'

He took her chin in his hand.

'Paula, you must. I can't ask you to wait around. I'm not in a position to make any promises.'

Her eyes misted.

'I'll wait anyway. I'll always be here for you. Tell me what's troubling you.'

'This is about as serious as it gets. Once you know then you must erase every word I've said from your mind. If you slip up and say something accidentally, you could ruin everything. I'm banking on your vigilance and loyalty.'

'And my love.'

He loved her, too, but he couldn't say it.

'You must tell no-one.'

She pulled herself up straight and whispered, her voice ragged, 'You have my word, Beau. I promise I will not let you down.'

A hush came over the room; a stillness as he prepared to speak. Paula moved closer.

'What is it? Tell me.'

His voice became a surreal whisper.

'It's Claire. Her life is in danger.'

'What?' Paula stifled a cry. 'In danger? You must be mistaken.'

'If only I were,' he said, resignation shafting through his words, 'but there's no mistake.'

'What have the doctors said? Is her

illness a result of the car accident? You mustn't give up hope. I'll be there for you. Please, I want to be there for her. You can't shut me out. You heard her earlier. I mean a lot to her.'

He caught her hands to him.

'Paula! We mustn't wake Claire. She has no idea about any of this. There's nothing you can do to help.'

There was sorrow, sweet sorrow in her eyes when she gazed up at him and nodded.

'Beau, you haven't given up hope. We can't give up hope.'

'Claire isn't sick and you can be sure I haven't given up hope, but I can't say any more. I've probably said far too much. The less you know, the safer the secret. I've only trusted you with this much to explain my cold, indifferent behaviour towards you, and why you can't continue to see Claire or me. It's not what I want. It's been forced on me.'

Paula couldn't take it in.

'It doesn't make sense. If Claire's not

ill . . . Please, why can't I see her in the future? If she's in danger, she's going to need me . . . a woman.'

He cupped her face into his hands, searched questioningly into her eyes.

'Please, Paula, don't pressure me. Forget what I've said and never betray the trust I've placed in you.'

'Of course I won't. I've given my word. But how can I forget it? If you really trusted me, you'd tell me the full story. I'm going to worry about you and Claire. Why is her life in danger?' Her eyes wide, she raised her voice, 'Are you saying someone has threatened to kill her?'

'No. I'm beginning to think I made a mistake telling you anything. Question time's over.'

But Paula's mind was already busy filtering through the possibilities. She couldn't help it, and one stood out.

'Someone's threatened to kidnap Claire, haven't they?'

There was a flicker of recognition in his eyes as he stood up. She drew in her breath, knowing she had her answer.

'Beau, how could the beast? You've both been through so much. I don't know what to say.'

'Damn it all, Paula, you don't have to say anything. The world's full of people who'll do anything for money. Anything.'

'You're being blackmailed, aren't you? If you don't pay up they've threatened to kidnap Claire. That's really serious stuff. We'll inform the police immediately. We'll pretend to pay the ransom, and then . . . I remember a case . . . '

'Stop it, stop probing. You're not involved,' he ground out. 'I've said my last word on the subject. Enough that you understand why I've turned my beautiful island into a fortress, and it's off-limits to people, particularly the prying media, and why your chronic curiosity has been such a pain in the butt.'

He gestured helplessly with his hands.

'Beau, I'm terribly sorry. Are you expecting things to happen soon?' she asked quietly, rising, going to his side, anxious to comfort him.

'I'm negotiating.'

He edged away.

'Negotiating? You're going to pay the ransom? You have told the police?'

He shook his head.

'The inquisition is over.'

'I'm grateful you've trusted me. Very.'

She placed her hand gently on his arm, gazed up at him, and felt him jerk away from her.

'Don't, Paula. It's torture being near you and not holding you. I need you in my arms like crazy.'

His voice was husky with passion, his eyes as dark, as fiery as sapphires. He moved aggressively to stand by the fire. She faced him; her voice trembled.

'You love me, Beau. You can't go on denying it for ever. Hold me, please?'

'Damn it, you bewitching temptress.'

He reached out to her. She came quickly into his arms. His lips covered hers, and immersed her in a world of sensuality. His kiss deepened.

'Paula, my dearest one,' he murmured as they drew apart.

She linked her fingers behind his head and at last surrendered to the joy of knowing with certainty that he loved her. And then came a small cough. Claire, bleary-eyed, her long dark hair curling about her pink cheeks, stood in the doorway. Hastily they separated.

'Gosh, it's awfully quiet in here,' the child said rubbing her eyes.

Paula hurried to her side.

'Were you two kissing?' she asked.

Paula glanced across at Beau. He was grinning.

'We may have been,' he said. 'But, possum, it's time we went home.'

Claire nodded and yawned.

'I wouldn't mind, Daddy. I love Paula, too.' And then holding out her right arm, she jangled her bracelet. 'Her present is awesome.'

'Awesome?' Beau asked. 'Where do you get these expressions?'

Paula and Claire joined hands and laughed.

'I'll get Claire into her clothes while you load up the car,' Paula suggested.

Soon Beau returned with a warm blanket and wrapped it about Claire's shoulders.

'Daddy, can our next picnic be on the island?' she asked. 'I want to show it to Paula because she's a townie and I know all the interesting places and the animals.'

Standing behind the child, he replied, 'Yes, we must arrange something.'

But even as he spoke, he was shaking his head, signalling to Paula that it would not happen.

'Now, say thank you to Paula,' he said, as he took his daughter's hand, and they moved to the front door.

So their goodbye had finally come.

'It's been wonderful today.'

She paused to halt the tell-tale tremor in her voice.

'Have you enjoyed yourself, Claire?'

Claire nodded.

'It's been grouse.'

'Grouse? Is that another word Paula's taught you?'

'Yes, and it means even better than good, Daddy.'

'Then it's certainly been grouse, but I don't think Miss Hines will approve the expression.'

He smiled as he bent to kiss Paula on the forehead, at the same time tucking a note into her hand.

'Good-night, and thanks for a lovely . . . I mean a grouse day,' he said.

She clutched at the note as the heat of his nearness, the ache of desire, swept over her. Her cheek throbbed where his lips had touched her.

'Thank you,' she whispered.

Gathering Claire in his arms, he turned towards the gate before looking over his shoulder to call, 'We'll be in touch.'

'Safe journey home.'

She raised her arm in farewell. He would not have seen her wave, for the moon had forsaken her, standing forlorn in her little garden. The two people she loved were gone. She shivered and hurried inside, his note clenched tightly in her hand. Anxiously, she unfolded it.

One day, it read, *all this will be over. If you are still here I will come for you. But you have your own life to live, so don't wait around.*

Paula had no doubt that she would be in Acacia Bay, no matter how long it took for him to come for her.

Back on his island, Beau felt at ease for the first time since Paula had come into his life. He'd been wrong about her from the beginning. She was no threat to him or to Claire, and once the blackmailers were caught, if she was still in the Bay, he'd go to her.

As he thought of her, a stab of longing powered through his body. He desired her, but his feelings went much deeper than that. Beneath her engaging impertinence, her vitality, lay a warm, gentle and open person. He had fought against loving her as full on as he might fight an international takeover of one of his companies. But in his heart he knew he was always going to lose.

For now, though, he had to play the waiting game. Everything must appear normal. Soon, he hoped, the black-mailer would make his move. The police had advised it was one thing to suspect who the culprit was, another to prove it. He must be caught in the act.

His loyal staff had never questioned his orders when he informed them that, without Claire's knowledge she had to be constantly watched and no-one should come on to the island without a clearance from him. It was possible, he explained, his wife's family in England might try to return his daughter to her former home without his permission. It was a variation on the truth. Only the detectives knew the full story.

Days turned to weeks, and during the long days and longer nights he yearned to talk to Paula, to confide his feelings for her, to unburden his fears and his uncertainties.

* ★ ★

It was a Sunday morning, and in winter sunshine, Paula was working in the garden, preparing for Maggie's return. As she pruned the roses, a siren sounded and a police car sped by. She stopped, secateurs poised, and recognised Sergeant Haldane behind the wheel.

Weeks ago, she'd have been in her car and on Haldane's tail in a flash, after a story, but she'd lost her appetite for the chase. Anyway, it was probably only a squabble over stall positions at the monthly art and craft market.

Avoiding the thorns, she placed the rose clippings into the garden barrow and was wheeling it along the side of the house when, through the open window, she heard the phone ring. It switched to automatic answering, and she continued on her way to the back of the house. It wasn't until she was bagging the clippings for collection that she made the connection between the police siren and her call. Hurrying inside, she dragged off her gloves and activated the answering machine.

'Paula, I'm at the office. Get down here as soon as possible. Something big's been happening over at the island,' Joe's voice bawled out.

It took a minute or two for her to react. Somehow the kidnap threat had always seemed unreal. Now it wasn't. Dear God, please let it fail, she prayed as she grabbed up her bag and tape recorder, and headed for the office.

'What's happened Joe?' she gasped.

'There's been a kidnap attempt on the island.'

'I'm going around to the police station immediately. I must find out if Claire's safe.'

'You know it's the kid?' Joe rasped.

Paula sucked in her breath. It had slipped out so easily.

'It's always a defenceless child, or a woman, isn't it?'

Joe stared at her.

'Are you keeping something from me?'

'Later, Joe,' Paula choked out. 'I have to get to the station.'

'I need you here to monitor the phone.'

'I'll take the pictures,' she protested, her voice rising dangerously.

'The police know me. I'm a local. They're more likely to talk to me. Calm yourself, girl.'

'But you don't understand. I knew there would be an attempt on Claire's life. Beau told me. That's why the island's been locked up like a prison. He was being blackmailed. I haven't got all the facts, but I know a bit of the background.'

It came pouring out like a river in flood, all the information, so long pent up, so needed to be shared. Paula hadn't intended it; it just happened. She was sweating, hot with emotion, her nerve ends jangling.

'Well, you kept real quiet about it, didn't you?'

'I swore not to say anything,' she snapped. 'Now can I go?'

'No. You're too emotional. Get out that historical piece you were doing on the island, knock it into shape as a feature. We can run it with the story. Look out some pictures to go with it.'

'You can't do this to me.'

'Tough. I'm doing it.'

She folded her arms across her body.

'And while you're chasing the story of the year, is there anything else I can do?'

'Sure. You reckon you've got all the info. Do a background piece on Powers.'

'No way. Beau told me in confidence. I am not going to dig up a lot of dirt from the Powers' past. It has nothing to do with the kidnap.'

'It might. Write what you know.'

'You promise to call the minute you hear anything?'

Paula flopped into a chair as Joe departed, and let out a long, anguished cry.

'It's not fair, it's not fair.'

After making a mug of strong, black coffee, she keyed into the computer and brought the article about the island on to the screen. She read and re-read it, broke it into smaller features, and phoned the local conservation group chairman to get details of the island's environmental importance.

Time hardly seemed to move. Joe didn't ring. The urge to write overtook her, and soon her fingers tapped out a piece detailing the fact that the island has been closed to visitors and tight security measures taken since its owner resumed residence.

Why, she speculated as she wrote. Because the kidnap attempt was expected? The family was being blackmailed and when Powers didn't pay up, the threat to kidnap the child followed. Why was the family being blackmailed? Was the death of Powers' wife significant?

As she read it back, she realised that writing it had helped get her through the terrible waiting period. She also realised there was still much she didn't understand about the abduction threat. The phone shrilled into her thoughts. Joe was at the other end.

'It happened early this morning. The child's safe, and two people have been taken into custody for questioning. Haldane is bringing them back from the island later today. I can't tell you any more, except they say it was a pretty amateurish attempt.'

Paula's heart pounded wildly.

'Claire's safe,' she said on a long sigh.

'I'll hang around here for a while in case anything else breaks. We'll bring out a special four-page edition tomorrow morning.'

Her heart did a double take. Beau would hate it.

'Excuse me? A special edition? You'd risk Powers' wrath? Besides, without ads we can't afford it.'

'The media will be swarming down here in an hour or two. An attempted child kidnap is big news. Given a choice, who would he want to be the first to tell the real story?'

She paused.

'Us, I guess.'

'We've got credibility and some integrity. And with your inside information we'll get it right.'

'Do you know whom they've arrested? Locals?' she breathed.

'The police are tight-lipped, but they're not locals.'

When she hung up, an uneasy feeling stirred within her. Beau would hate any publicity. She closed her eyes and tried not to think about his reaction. She had a job to do. Hastily she re-read her work, operated the printer, and placed the copy on Joe's desk with a selection of historical photos of the island.

Joe had said they'd learn the identity of the kidnappers soon enough, but his soon enough wasn't soon enough for her. Paula was through with waiting. Soon she was driving towards the island, planning her moves as she went.

Parking her car a short walk from the

bridge, she slung the camera bag over her shoulder, and moved cautiously forward. As she expected, the approach to the bridge was cordoned off, and a uniformed policeman patrolled the area. A helicopter circled overhead.

Dodging furtively between bushy outcrops and trees she found a rotting old jetty which gave her cover. Using the right camera lens and settings, she was close enough to zoom in on the bridge. She settled down to wait.

The minutes turned to an hour. Cold and uncomfortable, dampness seeped into her shoes. How long, she wondered, before the police vehicle came rattling across the bridge from the Hall.

Her nose itched. She glanced at her watch. It was after three and she hadn't eaten for hours. Her tummy rumbled so loudly she feared the policeman on duty might hear it. Then a police siren sounded, followed by the rattling of a car over the bridge planks. The policeman removed the cordon. Tense, she stood, rested the camera on an old pylon and focused it. At exactly the right time the sun broke through the watery sky and her wait ended.

The car gathered speed immediately it left the bridge and disappeared into the distance, its siren shrieking. Paula had fired the camera several times, and, yes, she'd recognised one of the abductors. The aloof woman with the lustrous black hair and arched eye-brows, who sat in the back of the car, was Olivia!

Questions tumbled over in her mind as she made her way back to her car, slipped out of her damp shoes and drove to the office.

Why would Olivia kidnap her own niece? Didn't the woman come from a wealthy family? Paula desperately wanted to see Beau, to hold and comfort him, to tell him she loved him, to understand.

Joe was pounding with two fingers on the keyboard when she got to the office. He looked up, noted her muddy shoes in one hand, and touching his glasses down his nose, growled, 'Didn't I tell you to stay put?'

'Have you seen Beau or Claire?' Her voice quivered. 'Are they all right?'

'Don't you listen to anything I say? They're in good spirits according to the police but they're staying put on the island for a day or two.'

'What happened? What actually happened, Joe?'

'I hope you're not going to get sick on me again.'

'Joe,' she cried, 'what happened?'

'The authorities expected the kidnap. They were pretty sure they were dealing with amateurs, but had to catch them at it before they could lay any charges. The police aren't saying much, and damn it all, I missed getting a picture of them arriving at the station because they were taken in via the back alley.'

'I can tell you who one of them is,' Paula spat out.

'Yeah?'

'Beau's sister-in-law, Olivia.'

Joe whistled.

'His sister-in-law! Daughter of a lord? You're sure?'

'One hundred per cent.'

He put up his hand.

'Don't tell me your source. So long as you can guarantee it.'

'I couldn't be more certain.'

'Well, what're you waiting for? Get it down. It'll make great copy. The issue's going to be a ripper.'

'You're not the least concerned for the Powers' family?' she asked.

'Of course I am, but I can live with that. For the first time we have the chance to scoop the national papers and put ourselves on the map. It's what your father expects of me.'

'It's exactly what Dad expects, but since when have you allowed him to dictate editorial policy? Weren't you defending Beau's privacy only weeks ago?'

'Things are different now,' he growled.

She turned away, uncomfortable, avoiding the next question, before realising she still held her camera in her hand.

'Oh, while you're at it, can we get this developed?'

Paula wound on the film, removing it from the camera as she spoke.

'There might be something useful on it.'

'Such as?'

'Such as a picture of Olivia and her male accomplice in the police car.'

Joe stared at her.

'Fair dinkum! You're your father's daughter, no question.'

'No question,' she snapped, making her way to her work station, revolting against the fact that as a reporter she was obliged to do her job, for her mind crowded with arguments against everything she was about to write.

Heavy-hearted, Paula switched on her machine and began keying in the story.

Although police have not yet named the two people who attempted to kidnap Claire Powers, the only child of Mr Beaumont Powers, a reliable source has identified one of them as the child's aunt, sister of the late Mrs Beaumont Powers.

As she included sketchy details of Olivia's stay on Beaumont Island, she questioned her actions. Would Beau understand? He would if he truly loved her. She sneezed almost non-stop as she handed Joe her copy.

'Good work, now push off, and don't come to work tomorrow unless you're feeling better. Your father will be proud of you,' Joe said.

Yes, her father would be proud, but the knot in her stomach tightened. At home, after a quick snack, Paula took a hot shower and climbed into bed. When the phone rang, she grabbed at the receiver. It was Beau!

'Paula, sweetheart.'

'Beau.'

Her heart began to sing.

'I can't talk long. I wanted you to know we're safe. I feel free for the first time in months. I'll get back to you as soon as I can.'

'I hope they lock up Olivia and throw

128

away the key,' she burst out.

'You know it was Olivia? The police promised not to release names overnight. Her family in England . . . '

He sounded cautious, and Paula felt uncomfortable.

'It wasn't hard to work out, Beau, but I don't understand why she'd want to kidnap Claire.'

'She's a big spender. She needs money to keep up her lifestyle.'

'Couldn't you have given her an allowance or something?'

'I tried that. I tried everything, but it wasn't enough. Her demands increased. It'll all come out eventually. I can't say too much now. The last thing I want is to have the story splashed over the media.'

Paula's discomfort increased. She had to tell him.

'You won't avoid the publicity, Beau. It's a major crime with an international flavour,' she said edgily.

'I realise that, but the only information the media gets will come from the police. They can't land on this island. Several choppers have been circling overhead, but there's no safe place for them to land.'

The knot in her stomach tightened.

'We're putting out a special edition.'

'You're what?' he thundered.

'We can't ignore it. The people around here have been phoning up. They want the facts, and we're in the best position to give them.'

'Well, tell Joe that's all they get — the facts. We'll talk in a day or two,' he ground out before hanging up.

Paula put down the phone, her heart heavy. First thing tomorrow she would somehow find her way out to the island and talk to him. They could never be completely happy together unless he recognised her obligations to her profession.

It was around eight in the morning when she made her way first to the pharmacy for tablets for what she realised was a nasty attack of hay fever. Surprisingly, there were already many shoppers on the main street.

'Been making the news I see,' John James, the pharmacist, said as she entered the shop.

Several customers looked up. They appeared to be staring at her.

Puzzled, she asked, 'What makes you say that?'

'The kidnap story,' came the reply.

'Oh, you heard. A dreadful business, wasn't it?'

'It's shattering for a little community like Acacia Bay,' an older man chipped in.

Others pressed around him, nodding their agreement.

'You took some good photos. That action shot of the kidnappers in the police car has everyone speculating about who the woman is. Her face has been blanked out, but most money is on Mr Powers' sister-in-law. Sometimes she bought a few things in town.'

Paula's mouth remained open as the comments ranged around her. She finally found space to speak.

'You mean you've seen the paper?'

'A bundle of them were on the doorstep when I arrived. People were already queueing for it when I opened this morning.'

He nodded to a small pile of papers on a chair.

'Joe advertised it over the local radio last night.'

Paula walked across to the bundle and reached for a copy, her hand trembling. All she could see were two pictures. The rest, the headlines, the copy, was a blur. One picture was of Beau in formal clothes. The caption read: **Was Mr Beaumont Powers thinking of the kidnap threat when this picture was taken by journalist Paula Bannister at the recent ball given on the island for the Blind Foundation volunteer workers?**

The other was of herself and Claire, taken on the day of their picnic. Dear heaven, her mind screamed, where did Joe get the pictures? What was Beau going to think when he saw them? That she'd betrayed him! The colour drained from her face. She shoved the paper under her arm and hurried from the shop. Every word, every picture would damn her in Beau's eyes. It was all there in print, even the speculative piece she'd written for her own therapy.

7

It was seven o'clock and Beau and Claire were at breakfast when Josh came in with a newspaper in his hand.

'Here's a copy of the special edition of 'The Standard'. I picked it up early at the newsagent like you said, Mr Powers.'

'Is that Paula's paper, Daddy?'

After all these weeks, Claire's face still lit up when Paula's name was mentioned. Ordinarily he would have been delighted. The barrier to their relationship was over, Olivia and her accomplice, Lorenzo Costa, had been charged. But after he'd spoken to Paula last night, his doubts about her integrity had returned to torture him. And later they had intensified when he heard the radio announcement that a special edition of 'The Standard' would bring up-to-the-minute details of the foiled kidnap attempt, exclusive pictures and a history of Beaumont Island.

'Yes, it's Paula's paper,' he said, accepting the copy from Josh, but carefully averting his eyes from it.

If there were any surprises he didn't want Claire around to hear his reaction.

'When can we see her again? Is she back?'

After the picnic, to explain her absence, he'd told his daughter that Paula had been recalled to Melbourne, but the child had asked daily when she was returning. And Claire still wasn't aware of the drama of yesterday. Briefly he'd explained that someone tried to land illegally on the island and the police were called to arrest them. It was his intention to sit down quietly with her this morning and relate as much as he could to his daughter without unduly disturbing her.

Tucking the newspaper under his arm, Beau went to Claire's side and stroked her hair.

'I'll ring the office today and enquire

if Paula's back. But don't get your hopes up. Her home and her family are in Melbourne. Now finish off your toast and juice. Miss Hines will be here to collect you. I'll be in my study if anyone needs me.'

He kissed her forehead and strode from the room. Outside, his shoulders slumped. He could already see on the front page the unforgivable — a picture of his daughter with Paula — a picture she'd asked him to take on the day of the picnic.

At the door of his study he removed keys from his pocket and unlocked it. He hurled it to and proceeded to his desk where, in one quick motion, he swept everything aside. Spreading out 'The Standard' he perched uneasily on the edge of his chair.

It was a good picture of him. Until this moment he hadn't realised how good Paula was at her job. He'd surrounded the Hall with security people at that cursed charity ball, yet she'd managed to get the photograph without his knowledge. She'd even tricked him into taking pictures of her with his daughter. She was a shrewd, ambitious operator.

What a fool he'd been, falling for her innocent eyes and her line about caring for Claire. And last night when he talked to her by phone, she hadn't mentioned the photographs. He fisted his hands.

How was he going to tell his daughter the truth about the woman she'd grown so close to? He crushed the paper into a tight ball and hurled it to the other side of the room. It was only eight o'clock, but he couldn't wait. He picked up the phone and tapped out 'The Standard' number . . .

Paula stormed into the newsroom brandishing the special edition.

'Is this your idea of a sick joke, Joe?' she cried, throwing the paper on her desk.

Joe swivelled around on his chair looked up and frowned. There were dark and swollen pockets under his eyes, but this wasn't the time to start feeling sorry for him.

'I thought congratulations might be in order,' he growled.

'The pictures on the front page. Who gave you permission to use them?'

And then, like a flash, she remembered. Joe didn't know she'd taken the shot of Beau without his agreement. As for the one of herself and Claire, how did that get into Joe's hands?

'I'm the editor. You took the photos but you don't own them.'

'Problem is, Powers didn't know I took that picture of him. It was a spur-of-the-moment thing. He had no idea.'

'And the other picture of you with his daughter? Who took that?'

'He did, but not for the paper. How did you get it, Joe?'

'It was on the reel of film you gave me for processing last night with the picture of the kidnappers.'

She couldn't believe her carelessness.

'Dear heaven, I completely forgot

about it. But you must have realised it was personal.'

He shrugged. 'You gave it to me.'

She slapped her hand to her head.

'This is awful. I must get out to the island, and explain things to Beau before he sees the paper.'

She picked up the phone with a shaky hand, but Joe wrestled it from her, replacing it in its cradle.

'You're too late. He's seen it already.'

Paula stared at him.

'He's seen it? But how?'

'Don't ask me.'

'I wanted to talk to him before he had a chance to read the paper. I wanted to apologise, to make him understand. Now,' she wailed, 'it'll be all over for us.'

'I'm not going to pretend I understand what's going on between you two. All I know is that Powers wants to speak to you immediately. He left a phone number.'

He handed her a piece of paper.

'I told him the special edition was my

idea, but do you reckon I could convince him? No way. It seems I don't get credit for anything around here these days.'

Paula's shoulders tightened. She reached for the back of a chair to support herself.

'You told him, but he still blames me? He thinks it was my idea?'

'You've got it. He can't believe an old hack like me has a special edition in him, I reckon.'

She seized Joe's arm.

'How can I convince him that I didn't know you would use the pictures?'

'We all make mistakes. He'll calm down. It's a two-day wonder anyway.'

'I don't think so.'

Then, she had another terrifying thought.

'Joe, you haven't promised any of those picture negatives to the dailies?'

'You don't have to be my conscience, too, Paula.'

'Beau distrusted me from the beginning and now . . . ' She lifted her shoulders. 'I don't blame you. I've been foolish, but my by-lines are plastered all over the paper, aren't they?'

'A man can't win. If I hadn't attributed the pictures and stories to you, you'd have gone ballistic. Can we talk about this later? I've done a twenty-four hour shift. Everyone else's gone home and I'm on my way. You're in charge.'

'Joe, if only you'd consulted me about by-lines and those personal pictures,' she called out to his departing figure, causing him to swing around.

'Like you consulted me about the real reason you're in Acacia Bay?'

Her eyes widened, her heart beat stalled.

'You know then? I'm truly sorry. I wanted to talk to you about it, but Dad thought if you knew I was checking the paper's viability you'd worry, perhaps needlessly.'

'Your dad told me it had to start making a profit, or it goes under. Why do you think I pulled out all stops on this special edition? To make people stand up and take notice of 'The Standard', that's why. The local rag's an important part of this community, and if you try to take it from us, you'll have a real fight on your hands.'

'I don't want to take it from you. I'm on your side. Go home, Joe. You're tired. We'll talk about it tomorrow.'

The building fell eerily silent. Paula turned over the note on which Beau's phone number was written. Eventually she'd have to call him, but how to make him listen and understand?

She'd let everyone she cared about down, including Joe. Beau had asked for her trust and she'd given it without question. Events had simply caught up with her, and turned that promise into what now, on the surface, seemed like a betrayal. If only she hadn't taken that photograph in a fit of defiance. But going over everything, rationalising, provided no answers. She had to talk to Beau.

Hurrying to the cloakroom, she

rinsed her hands, dashed cool water over her hot cheeks, ran a brush through her hair and lightly applied fresh make-up. She didn't feel better, but she looked it.

As she walked slowly back to the news-room, a draught of cool air dislodged her hair. She shivered. Straightening her shoulders, she stepped resolutely into the room. A slight sound sent her heart pumping erratically. Joe's chair swung around to face her. Leaping backwards, she uttered a cry of alarm.

Beau was lounging in the seat, his arms crossed over his black leather jacket, his long legs encased in jeans, untamed hair curled on to his forehead. A ray of sunlight through the window picked up his dark, chiselled jawline, the weariness under his eyes. But it was his icy gaze which momentarily suspended her footsteps, until her impetuous heart insisted on having its way. She ran to him.

'Beau, my dearest love, it's over and little Claire's safe. I've been out of my mind with worry these last few weeks.'

'Keep your distance.'

Like the volley of a pistol, his words halted her. His eyes darkened. He straightened in the chair, as if gearing up for something. She clutched at a nearby desk for support, her breath coming in short stabs.

'Beau, you're angry. I'm terribly sorry. I know I've let you down,' she began, dragging locks of hair back over one ear, 'but not intentionally. I can explain.'

He remained silent, his lips locked tightly, his only movement a pulse throbbing in his neck. Paula sank on to the desk.

'Say something, Beau, anything, but don't shut me out.'

'I'm waiting for your explanation.'

He eased back into the chair and began to swivel across and back, across and back, the muscles working in his thighs visible through the denim of his jeans. She stumbled over her words.

'I don't know where to begin.'

'Start with the photographs.'

'It wasn't meant to happen.'

His chair spun full on, stopped. He leaned forward.

'Joe tried to take the blame for you, but I noticed you got all the by-lines. You took the pictures.'

'Please try to understand. I know this looks like unethical journalism, but it's not. I dislike that kind of reporting as much as you.'

'I don't dislike it. I despise it.'

'I'm wasting my breath, aren't I? You've already condemned me.'

'Can you convince me otherwise?' he sneered.

'For goodness' sake, stop swivelling. I can't think.'

'You never think. That's your problem. You rush headlong into things.'

'I admit I sometimes get a bit carried away. My father calls it enthusiasm.'

'I call it arrogant disregard for people's feelings.'

He glanced at his watch.

'I haven't got all day. If you have any

kind of defence, get on with it.'

The palms of her hands locked tightly together as she tilted her chin and looked directly into his eyes.

'I was horrified when I saw the photos on the front page. I had no idea Joe intended to use them. I was at home with a severe attack of hay fever.'

He raised one supercilious brow.

'Do you deny taking the picture of me, and fooling me into taking one of you and Claire?'

She nodded miserably.

'I took your photo at the ball on impulse, but not for publication. As for the one of the picnic, of course it wasn't meant for the paper. When I handed the spool to Joe, I forgot it was on the same roll of film I shot the police car taking Olivia and her accomplice to the station. I was horrified to see it in print.'

Beau raised his shoulders, tilted his head.

'You were under instructions not to photograph any of my household the night of the ball. Your arrogance astounds me.'

'I'm desperately sorry, Beau, but I can't change the past. You'd been unpleasant to me that night, you watched me like a hawk, I'd finished my job. It was a bit of a challenge. I really expected you to notice the flash and make a scene, but you didn't. If I hadn't been taken ill that night, Joe wouldn't have known the negatives existed. Do you never make mistakes in your business dealings?'

'I'd be broke if I'd made as many as you.'

His eyes narrowed. Casually he crossed his legs, leaned farther back in the chair.

'I don't believe a word you're telling me.'

Her protests were futile. He wasn't going to give her a fair hearing.

'I don't have to listen to this,' she said with quiet determination as she began walking back to the corridor.

This time the fight was over for keeps.

She heard him rise, his footsteps heading for the outer entrance. The ache in her heart told her to call him back, but her pride kept her going. She felt a chill as the door slammed shut.

Paula returned to the newsroom and slumped into the chair where he had sat. It retained his body warmth, the faint scent of him. She huddled into its depth as if to recapture the essence of the man, and told herself she was not going to cry. But the tears came. And she gave way to her grief.

The phone rang insistently, until Paula could ignore it no longer. Wiping away the last of her tears she answered it.

'Are you all right, Paula? You sound a bit odd,' her father asked gruffly.

She sighed. 'Dad, I'm fine.'

'Congratulations on the special edition.'

'You're talking to the wrong person. It was Joe's idea — his reaction to you telling him the paper has to make a profit or you're closing it. I'm furious with you. Why didn't you let me speak to him first? He probably thinks I'm a modern day traitor.'

'Joe was suspicious, Paula. He asked me straight out what my plans were for the future. I've decided to amalgamate the paper with one of the nearby weeklies so you won't be needed down there after next week.'

'You're what?'

Her fighting spirit came to her in a rush. There was no way she'd let Joe and Acacia Bay down.

'I'm sorry to disappoint you, but I'm sticking around to see 'The Standard' doesn't go under. It's a paper with a soul and the people in these parts will keep it.'

Again there was hesitation at her father's end. He was obviously weighing things up in his very sharp business head. She crossed her fingers.

'All right, let's see how much of the newspaper business you've learned while you've been down there. I'll give you three months to get it back in the black.'

'Six months,' she snapped. 'I need six months.'

He sighed loudly, as if he were being indulgent.

'Very well, six months, on the condition that you promise to come home if you don't succeed. It's been ages since we spent time together.'

'You're on.'

She managed a smile. So something good had emerged out of the chaos of today.

'Thanks, Dad. You can be quite a lovable old bear when you want.'

'Don't go getting soft on me daughter. This is a business arrangement.'

Paula suspected that her tough old man had a tear in his voice.

'Well, good luck with the project. You make me very proud,' he added then hung up almost immediately.

'How'd you get on with Powers?' Joe asked next morning.

'The good news first. Dad's given us six months to turn the fortunes of the paper around. The bad news is Beau Powers wouldn't listen to me.'

'You fell for him, eh? He'll get over it, Paula. When he's thought about it a while, he'll realise the chain of circumstances. You were only doing your job.'

She shook her head.

'It's finished. If he rings here, I don't want to speak to him. Now, let's get down to planning the revival of 'The Standard'.'

It was Thursday when Joe brought the cheque to her desk after lunch.

'What do you reckon we ought to do with this?' he asked, handing it to her.

She blinked.

'What on earth? Ten thousand dollars! Now who could be . . . '

She read on. When she saw the signature, she edged deeper into her chair to re-read it, to make sure.

Beau Power's cheque for ten thousand dollars was made out to 'The Standard'!

'How did this arrive, Joe?'

'By courier.'

'He didn't dare deliver it himself. He knew exactly the kind of reception he'd get. I presume there's a note with it.'

Joe handed her the sheet of quality white stationery. Grimly holding on to her cool, she skimmed through the contents.

'Who told him we had cash-flow problems?'

'Who tells the great man anything?'

'The cheque goes straight back, Joe. We're not a charitable institution. It's downright insulting. How dare he suppose we're not capable of making the paper pay?'

'No need to get huffy with me. I agree one hundred per cent with you. I'll return the cheque with a note.'

She was about to nod her agreement when an irresistible idea slipped into her mind.

'No! On second thoughts, I'll deliver it in person. It will give me a great deal of satisfaction to tell him what he can do with his money.'

'The island's still out of bounds.'

'I'd forgotten that. Blast!' Paula exclaimed.

'Ring first. I'm sure if you say who it is they'll make some arrangements to let you on.'

'I doubt it. Powers doesn't trust me. But I can try. We are doing the right thing returning the money, Joe, aren't we?'

'What else would we do with it?'

'Tear it up and forget it happened.'

She rested her finger at the side of her mouth and began to smile.

'Come to think of it, I might conduct that little ceremony in front of Mr Acacia Bay. This is one local project he isn't going to influence.'

'Paula, don't you go doing anything silly now.'

'Me do something silly? Come on, Joe.'

She grinned. Paula had thought of a way she could have the last laugh on Beau Powers.

8

Paula shoved the cheque into her wallet, tidied her desk and left. After changing into warm clothes and strong shoes at her cottage, she made her way to Don Hawkins' boat-shed, on the shore of the lake side of the island.

'I take it you've used one of these runabouts before?' Hawkins asked.

'Several times.'

She crossed her fingers, for she hadn't been near a boat in years.

'But it was ages ago so I'll get you to start it for me and show me how to steer. They're all so different.'

She smiled up at him.

'Where's your fishing gear?'

'I'm not fishing. I'm with 'The Standard', doing a speculative piece on the potential for ferry trips across to the island when it reopens. You can't beat doing it yourself to discover the pitfalls.'

He led her to a moored boat, where he retrieved a life jacket and tossed it to her. As she put it on, she thought how small the boat looked, how vast the stretch of water.

'OK, you get in and I'll start the motor. I wouldn't let you go out on your own if the weather report wasn't good.'

'Thanks. Would you mind holding it steady for me, please?' she asked, climbing gingerly into it.

'Can do.'

With a lurch she plopped down beside the steering stick. Hawkins gave the runabout a push and it sallied forth.

'Enjoy yourself,' he called before disappearing into the boatshed.

Everything suddenly grew very still. There was no-one in sight, and the island looked a million miles away. Inside the boating shed, Don Hawkins picked up the phone and dialled Beaumont Hall.

'Josh, I thought you'd like to know, the young woman from the paper has just hired one of my boats and she's heading your way,' he said chuckling. 'You'd better keep an eye out for her. I don't think she knows much about sailing!'

How tiny the craft seemed to Paula. How high the water lapped against its sides. And how suddenly the shore seemed to fade into the distance, yet the island stayed no more than a speck on the horizon. As the boat motored farther from land, fingers of fear began to grip her heart. What on earth was she doing out here? If she got safely to the island, did tearing up the cheque in Beau's face achieve anything? Out here, alone beneath a leaden sky, she questioned why she always felt the necessity to prove something, first to her father and now to Powers.

She had to take a long, hard look at her life. She already knew what she'd see — a headstrong girl on a frenetic search for new experiences, a girl who, deep-down, yearned for a loving, stable influence in her life. For a brief time she thought that might have come from Beau. She shifted in her seat, tilted her chin, determined that she'd succeed in this final headstrong act.

The mist hung low. She shivered and wrapped her scarf more closely around her neck. Setting back her shoulders, she redoubled to her resolve to make it, and there suddenly out of the mist, as if a rush of optimism had brought it about, loomed Beaumont Hall. She took a long breath as a tremor of foreboding skipped along her spine. She'd made it.

As the boat drew closer to the shore, she silenced the motor, swung her bag across her shoulders and leaped into the shallows, the moor rope in hand. But the mudflats at the water's edge sucked at her shoes and dragged her down. The rope fell from her hand. She was floundering, hardly able to move. Flinging her bag on to the shore, she struggled to free herself. The last thing she wanted to do was call for help.

An overhanging branch was inches

away. She reached for it, and suddenly strong, hard fingers gripped her wrists. Beau crouched on the hillock, shifted his hold adroitly to beneath her arms and effortlessly lifted her free. She gasped, unable to speak, as he sat her on firm ground.

She needed to be angry with him for discovering her, but his closeness blanked out everything else. The weeks of their separation, her attempts to put him out of her life had failed miserably. She still loved him. The ache of losing him had always lain close to the surface.

'Thanks,' she mumbled, as he dragged off her shoes and socks.

'So you made it.'

Why wasn't he demanding to know what she was doing on his island or accusing her of lying, or snooping? She searched for something coherent to say, but only came up with, 'I wasn't expecting a welcoming committee.'

'It was lucky I was in the area. You might still have been struggling in the mud.'

'Lucky? Or were you expecting me?'

'I was expecting you.'

'Who told you?' she asked through chattering teeth.

'Later. Let's get you inside for a warm shower and a drink.'

Alarmed, she jumped to her feet.

'Certainly not.'

'I can't have you getting another chill on my island. You'll give it a bad name. Come on! We're wasting time here.'

She hated to give in, but he brought a smile to her lips, eased the tension.

'All right, but only for a hot drink.'

Without another word, he swung her into his arms, leaving her speechless with surprise. He held her strongly, securely at first and then with gentle intimacy as he gazed down at her. It would have been so easy to let him take over, but she'd been in his arms before and it had led only to heartache and emptiness. It mustn't happen again.

'Please put me down,' she insisted.

'Very well, but I don't advise it with bare feet. It's rough and there are creepy crawlies, snakes.'

'OK. You win, but don't go getting any ideas.'

'What did you have in mind?'

She warned herself not to get too comfortable, though her arms naturally linked behind his neck.

'Don't you want to know why I'm here?'

'It can wait until you get out of your wet clothes.'

'I haven't got an invitation. Are you sure it's all right for someone you don't trust to enter your house?' she taunted.

'Will you stop rabbiting on?'

Beau felt anxious, afraid he might say or do something to spoil everything. He'd waited for what seemed an eternity, to see her again, to seek her forgiveness. He couldn't afford to blow it now. She was such a gutsy little thing, shivering with the cold, but still showing plenty of bravado.

'We'll talk inside,' he said.

'What about?'

'Us.'

When she raised wide eyes, he realised his simple answer had stunned her. Whatever happened, he couldn't let her turn back on him. This would be his last chance to square things with her.

'Paula, there's so much I want to say to you.'

She gave up the struggle more easily than he had expected.

'You're right. We should talk.'

He gazed down on her. In the dewy onset of evening, her eyes seemed to sparkle. She was so lovely, it almost frightened him. He drew her closer.

'Please, Beau, don't do this,' she whispered.

'What?'

He pushed aside a tendril of hair from her face.

'Don't hold you? Don't kiss you? Why not, Paula?'

He cupped her chin with his hand, made her eyes meet his, saw the response and felt easier.

'Because for you it's some kind of game. You've never really cared enough about me, or you'd have trusted me, believed in me.'

'I do, Paula. That's what I want to tell you.'

He felt her tremble. They were inside the Hall.

'You can put me down now,' she said coldly.

She didn't believe him. He set her on her feet, knowing he still had a lot of work to do to convince her. She was glancing down at her clothes.

'What a mess,' she said disdainfully.

'A delightful mess.'

To him she appeared waif-like, vulnerable, her wind-tossed hair curling about her forehead, her clothes water-stained. But she no longer deceived him with her little-girl look. She was all woman.

'How's Claire? Did she understand about the kidnap threat beforehand?' she asked as they reached the staircase.

'She sensed it. She can't wait to see you, by the way. She asks about you every day.'

'Oh! And you don't mind?'

'Of course I mind. Sometimes I think she loves you more than me.'

He averted his eyes, but then changed his mind.

'Paula, I'm grateful to you for pointing out that the most important gift I can give my child is my time. I've already started to cut down on business commitments.'

She reached out to him.

'That's super, Beau, but never doubt her love for you. You're her father, but I'm a woman, an only child and I understand her needs and, forgive me, her loneliness.'

'You're right, as usual.'

'Oh, come on.'

Her eyes sparkled with pleasure as he swung open the door of the study.

'There's a warm fire inside. We can talk without interruption in here,' he said.

She seemed reluctant. There was an edge to her voice.

'You don't lock it any more?'

'I had to lock it while Olivia was in the house. She was more than a little obsessed with my financial situation. Now, out of those clothes and into a shower.'

He slid aside a door to reveal a small bathroom.

'You'll find a wrap hanging on the peg. When you come out I'll get you a hot drink and we can talk.'

Paula carefully locked the door after she stepped into the en-suite. Soon the warmth of the water, the fresh, clean smell of body lotion foaming over her skin relaxed her and she stood, enjoying it, unwilling to think beyond the moment.

The robe hanging on the back of the door fitted well. She tied it across her waist before towelling her hair, and, uncertain, returned to Beau's study, carrying her damp clothes. He was sitting by the fire reading a newspaper. He looked up.

'Does that feel better?' he asked.

Nodding, she arranged the garments

on a chair by the fire.

'Why are you frowning?' he inquired.

'You said earlier you knew I was coming. How?'

There was a smile on his full lips.

'Can't you guess?'

Suddenly, as if a light had been switched on in her mind, she recalled the cheque.

'You sent that cheque . . . '

She rummaged in the pocket of her coat which lay on he chair, and drew it out.

'You knew I wouldn't take your money. You were hoping to lure me out here,' she cried. 'And I took the bait.'

He shrugged.

'What was a man to do? You wouldn't talk to me on the phone. I figured once you got the cheque, you'd come barn-storming over here to tick me off. But I thought you'd ring first. I didn't anticipate you'd do something as reckless as coming in a little runabout on your own. When I heard you were out on the water with the mist coming down . . . You could have drowned, Paula. It's very deep in places.'

Paula's teeth began to chatter. The enormity of what she'd done overwhelmed her. She found herself in his arms, her eyes glazed with tears.

'It was so scary, Beau. I promised myself out there I wouldn't do anything so crazy again.'

'Well, that's one thing we've settled.'

She ran her fist across her eyes.

'Sorry for unloading on you . . . '

'Any time. By the way, Don Hawkins at the boat-shed rang Josh to tell him you were on your way. I'd never have let anything happen to you.'

She punched him on the arm.

'I might have known. Anyway, now I'm here, let me perform what I came to do. 'The Standard' doesn't need hand-outs, Beau. Either we make a profit or we don't deserve to survive.'

Brandishing the cheque, she stood up.

'And this is what I think of your cheque.'

Tearing it into shreds she threw them into the fire. The heat curled and shrivelled them to ash in seconds.

'That feels better,' she said, as the sound of a knock came to the door and Mrs Marks entered bearing a tea tray.

'Thanks, Mrs Marks,' she said, though the housekeeper's lips remained pursed as Beau took the tray from her.

'She really likes you, Paula,' Beau said once she'd left. 'She's suggested more than once I should get in touch with that nice young reporter. It's just that you keep meeting her under strange circumstances.'

As he spoke, Beau poured her tea, buttered a scone for her, and placed them on the low table beside the settee.

'Sit down,' he ordered, 'and eat.'

He eased himself on to the chair beside her and held his lean hands to the flames.

'So, how's the paper going? Making some progress?'

She brushed a crumb from her mouth.

'We're getting there. Beau, is Claire really over the kidnap attempt?'

'She's doing all right. You know, the specialists said her sight might return once life settled down, and I had high hopes after we came home to Australia, until that damned Olivia showed up. I tried to protect my little girl. God knows I tried.'

'If her sight isn't damaged, we can give her a more stress-free life from now on, and who knows? You mustn't give up hope.'

'We? You and me?' he said simply. 'You and me?'

'Maybe.'

'What do you mean? Do you still love me?'

He lifted her chin so that their eyes met.

'Tell me, Paula.'

'How can my love survive when I know you don't trust me or respect my profession? When the pain of our last encounter still torments me?'

She drew her feet up under her, as if

shrinking from the memory.

'Don't close the door on me now, Paula. Say we have a chance.'

Paula's heart quickened, yet she dared not to hope.

'You mean a chance for a future together?'

'Yes, if you can forgive me. In the beginning, it was so easy to tell myself you were just another unscrupulous journalist flirting with me because you wanted an interview. How wrong I was.'

'Not altogether. I admit to a little flirting. You were so macho, so cold, yet simmering underneath with passion. I'd never met anyone so impossibly attractive before.'

'Paula, I'm trying to be serious.'

He slanted her a dry look, which brought the glimmer of a smile to her lips.

'So am I.'

'But my problem isn't only with journalists. You see I've mistrusted women for a long time. My wife, Helen, never really loved me. The marriage was a sham from the beginning.'

He sank into the cushions, his attention captured, it appeared, by memories.

'Yes, Beau,' Paula said gently, sitting beside him, 'go on. I'm listening.'

'You don't want the sordid details, but for Claire's sake we put on a public show of being happy for years. The day Helen was killed in the accident we'd had a fearful row about her behaviour. I told her to get out. She packed some of her belongings into the car and was on her way to her latest admirer's flat, with Claire, when it happened. Later, when a few media people rang for comments about the crash, I said some hasty things, and they were used to imply all kinds of untruths.'

He clenched one fist and punched it into his other hand. Paula's legs cramped beneath her but she let him go on talking.

'Not long afterwards, Olivia appeared on my doorstep saying I'd lose Claire if I didn't help her out with some debts.'

'But, Beau, you were the legal father. She couldn't take her from you.'

'She said Helen was pregnant when she married me, but wanted me because I had money. It had a ring of truth, but even if I wasn't Claire's biological father, I loved her too much to give her up. So, I offered Olivia an annual allowance. It was the quick, easy way to get rid of her.'

'That's when you decided to come home?' Paula murmured.

He nodded.

'I'd been thinking about it for ages. Claire needed peace and quiet. But I misjudged Olivia's tenacity. She followed us out here.'

'And made more demands?'

He continued slowly, his voice faltering occasionally.

'We settled here on the island and I had security fences and monitoring equipment installed, because I suspected Olivia might secretly steal back to England with Claire. I imagined long court battles, losing, the publicity. The last thing my daughter needed. Can you understand now why I seemed so paranoid?'

Fighting back tears, she took up his hand.

'What happened next?'

'She showed up again on the day of the ball, and so did a certain unknown reporter. I felt as if I were walking on hot coals. Over the next few days, while you were ill, Olivia and I talked. I gave her more money and warned her it was the last because I had blood tests to prove Claire was my child. They all confirmed she is mine.'

'You should have gone straight to the police.'

'And accuse Olivia of what? Asking for money? Besides, it would have resulted in more sensational publicity. I thought the woman would keep her promise to stay away, until the mysterious kidnap threats started to arrive. That's when I involved the police.'

'You suspected Olivia?'

'Sure, but the police pointed out that

wealthy parents, particularly if they've been in the news recently, are targets for extortionists. They couldn't rule out the idea that some low life was trying to screw me.'

He raked a hand through his hair.

'I suppose so, but it would have been a huge coincidence.'

'No bigger than the coincidence of you and Olivia arriving uninvited on the day of the ball. It was so awkward. I was expecting all those people. I thought I'd covered every contingency.'

'My timing couldn't have been worse.'

'Yes, you turned up in a vibrant blue dress which made your eyes seem alight, and a nose fairly itching to discover my secret. But I daren't let you get even a whiff of it.'

She slipped under his arm.

'How's my timing now?' she whispered, placing her lips to his cheek.

She tasted the salt of a tear, perhaps two, and looked into his magnificent blue eyes. They were soft, misty. Gently she dried the moisture from his cheeks with the pad of her finger.

'A man feels a bloody idiot,' he growled, drawing her nearer so that her head rested on his muscled chest.

'Beau, after those first intriguing hours on the island, my interest centred around you and Claire. I lost my appetite for a story. But I needed to understand why you were rejecting me.'

'That's what I thought on the day of the picnic, but then the kidnap attempt took place, my picture appeared in 'The Standard' and you wrote all that personal stuff. It threw me.'

'If only I hadn't taken that photograph,' she cut in, her voice rising. 'Everything happened so quickly after the news broke. Joe decided on a special edition. I knew my articles were included, but not the pictures of you and Claire.'

'When I saw the paper, I couldn't believe it.'

'I understand your anger. I planned to tell you face to face next day. I had no idea the paper would be out on the streets so early in the morning. That's the truth. I didn't know Joe would use the photos. Not that I could have stopped the issue. Joe did the right thing by 'The Standard' and the community, and you incidentally. It presented everything in a factual way.'

He placed a lean finger on her lips.

'Don't distress yourself. You're for-given. I let my anger get the better of me, and behaved badly. I hate myself for what I said to you at the office that day. You were only doing your job. I realised that after I calmed down. Is your heart generous enough to forgive me, Paula?'

'You have to trust me, Beau. Do you really trust me?'

'Yes, my darling, with my life and my daughter's life.'

'I think I came to Acacia Bay to fall in love.'

'Come here, sweetheart.'

He reached out to her, and, her heart turning somersaults with joy, she went to his side. He closed his arms about her and held her close.

'I love you, Paula. Will you marry me?' he whispered.

'Can we make it tomorrow?' she said against his broad chest, grinning.

'What's your hurry?'

'I'm moving out of Maggie's cottage at the weekend!'

There was a timid knock on the door, and a small voice called.

'Daddy, you said I could say hello to Paula before I went to bed. I've been waiting a really long time.'

'I guess we're going to put up with interruptions like this for a year or two,' he murmured into Paula's hair, before releasing her gently from his arms.

'I don't mind,' she replied, smiling.

She straightened her robe and ran her hand through her hair as she hurried to the door.

'Sunbeam,' she cried, wrapping her arms around the child, 'did you think I'd never come back?'

'Sometimes, Paula.'

'Your daddy and I have news for you. We hope you'll be pleased.'

'You sound happy. The room feels happy,' the child said beaming, glancing around as if she could see clearly.

Beau looked at Paula with raised brows, and then picked up his daughter.

'We're going to be married,' he said with laughing eyes. 'With your permission, of course.'

'It's just grouse! I always knew you loved Paula, Daddy.'

★   ★   ★

Paula moved to the window and gazed down upon the scene below. Acacia Bay residents were arriving on the island, taking up their open invitation to be at the wedding celebration and afterwards to enjoy a festive picnic and dancing on the lawns outside the Hall. She smiled wistfully, hardly daring to acknowledge that her wedding day had come. A tap on the door signalled the arrival of her father. It was time for the ceremony.

'You look beautiful. I wish your mother could have been here,' Paul Bannister said.

'Thanks, Dad. Me, too.'

Paula didn't know how her legs got her down the staircase, but soon they stood outside the ballroom, waiting for the cue to enter. She took a deep breath and fiddled with her bouquet. Her father squeezed her arm.

'Are you happy with my wedding present?'

'Ecstatic. I've always wanted to run my own newspaper and 'The Standard' is very special to me. So, are you happy with my present to you?'

'I didn't know I was getting one.'

'Your high-flying son-in-law and your ready-made granddaughter, of course. We're something we haven't been in a long while Dad — a family.'

Misty-eyed, she straightened his tie, though it needed no attention.

'Delighted, and I hope there'll be more grandchildren,' he said with a gleam in his eye.

'I think you can rely on it.'

At last the string quartet began playing the bridal march.

'Here we go, daughter.'

Paul crooked his arm for her and they entered the ballroom and began walking slowly down the aisle.

Beau couldn't believe how beautiful she looked. He turned to Claire, who stood beside him, clutching his hand.

'Paula's wearing a satin gown. It's got long sleeves and lots of pearls and buttons,' he said softly.

'I know, Daddy.'

He sucked in his breath.

'You can see it?'

'No, silly. She let me feel it. Tell me about her flowers,' Claire whispered.

He started breathing again. One day his daughter would see clearly. He had started to believe in miracles, for Paula had changed his life. She was part of him, embedded in his heart. She was his weakness and his strength.

Paula's gaze rested on Beau and

Claire as they stood, side by side. His eyes met hers. Even through her veil they connected. They had always connected.

He was a weaver of spells, he lit a fire in her, he was her weakness and her strength, and soon, her impetuous heart told her joyfully, he would be her husband.

THE END

We do hope that you have enjoyed reading this large print book.

Did you know that all of our titles are available for purchase?

We publish a wide range of high quality large print books including:
Romances, Mysteries, Classics
General Fiction
Non Fiction and Westerns

Special interest titles available in large print are:
The Little Oxford Dictionary
Music Book, Song Book
Hymn Book, Service Book

Also available from us courtesy of Oxford University Press:
Young Readers' Dictionary
(large print edition)
Young Readers' Thesaurus
(large print edition)

For further information or a free brochure, please contact us at:
Ulverscroft Large Print Books Ltd.,
The Green, Bradgate Road, Anstey,
Leicester, LE7 7FU, England.
Tel: (00 44) **0116 236 4325**
Fax: (00 44) **0116 234 0205**

Other titles in the
Linford Romance Library:

THE DOCTOR WAS A DOLL

Claire Vernon

Jackie runs a riding-school and, living happily with her father, feels no desire to get married. When Dr. Simon Hanson comes to the town, Jackie's friends try to matchmake, but he, like Jackie, wishes to remain single and they become good friends. When Jackie's father decides to remarry, she feels she is left all alone, not knowing the happiness that is waiting around the corner.

TO BE WITH YOU

Audrey Weigh

Heather, the proud owner of a small bus line, loves the countryside in her corner of Tasmania. Her life begins to change when two new men move into the area. Colin's charm overcomes her first resistance, while Grant also proves a warmer person than expected. But Colin is jealous when Grant gains special attention. The final test comes with the prospect of living in Hobart. Could Heather bear to leave her home and her business to be with the man she loves?

RUNAWAY HEART

Shirley Allen

Manuella's grandfather intends to marry her to the odious Don Miguel, and persuades her father to agree to the match. In desperation, Manuella, who is half-gypsy, runs away to her other family. When the gypsy camp is attacked by Don Miguel, her father and their followers, she is rescued by two Englishmen, Jonathan Wilde and Roderick Maine. Manuella falls in love with Roderick — but will he consider her suitable to be his wife?

FINGALA, MAID OF RATHAY

Mary Cummins

On his deathbed, Sir James Montgomery of Rathay asks his daughter, Fingala, to swear that she will not honour her marriage contract until her brother Patrick, the new heir, returns from serving the King. Patrick must marry. Rathay must not be left without a mistress. But Patrick has fallen in love with the Lady Catherine Gordon whom the King, James IV, has given in marriage to the young man who claims to be Richard of York, one of the princes in the Tower.

ZABILLET OF THE SNOW

Catherine Darby

For Zabillet, a young peasant girl growing up in the tiny French village of Fromage in the mid-fourteenth century, a respectable marriage is the height of her parents' ambitions for her. But life is changing. Zabillet's love for a handsome shepherd is tested when she is invited to join the La Neige household, where her mistress, Lady Petronella, has plans for her grandson, Benet. And over all broods the horror of the Great Death that claims all whom it touches.